HELL WEEK

BOOK 1

AMERICA FALLS

SCOTT MEDBURY

Copyright © 2020 Scott Medbury

All rights reserved. No part of this publication may be reproduced, distributed, or transmitted in any form or by any means, including photocopying, recording, or other electronic or mechanical methods, without the prior written permission of the publisher, except in the case of brief quotations embodied in critical reviews and certain other non-commercial uses permitted by copyright law.
All characters and events depicted in this work are fictitious. Any resemblance to real persons, living or dead is purely coincidental.

ISBN: 978-0-6450415-0-7

DEDICATION

This book is dedicated to Ian Medbury, thank you for showing me the importance of family. You're sorely missed Dad.

CONTENTS

1 Hell Breaks Loose - - - - - - - 7

2 We Hit the Road - - - - - - - 73

3 Encounters - - - - - - - - -135

4 Death Comes Calling - - - - - -183

ACKNOWLEDGMENTS

A big thank you to my wife Joanne for keeping me grounded and motivated. Thanks to all my "beta readers" and Janie Medbury for her insight and editing.

"Man is the cruelest animal."
— Friedrich Nietzsche

Part One

HELL BREAKS LOOSE

1

I don't think about death anymore, it takes too much energy, and God knows I need every bit of that. My name is Isaac Race. Both of my parents are dead and so is my sister, Rebecca. They were dead even before the attack. In fact, everyone I ever loved or cared about before is gone now. I can't complain too much though; the others have lost everybody too. All except the twins, Ben and Brooke… they have each other at least.

I guess I need to start at the beginning. Before the shit hit the fan, as my last foster father used to say all the time. Yes, I said my last foster father. I had two after my parents died. That's where I'll begin my story, just before the Pyongyang flu killed all the grown-ups… well, nearly all of them.

My Mom, Dad, and kid sister were killed in a house fire just before I turned 14. I wasn't at home that night; I'd stayed over at my best friend Tommy's house. It was a Saturday night and the cops and social workers all told me how lucky I was. I didn't feel lucky. For a long time, I kind of wished I'd been home. Maybe I could have saved them… or, if not, at least I would have died too. Surely that would have been better than the awful, empty feeling that is only now starting to fade.

If I'd died too, we would have been in Heaven together. Well, that's what I thought back then, when it first happened. I know there isn't a Heaven now. There can't be a Heaven without a God and I know there can't be a God, because no god could have let them do what they'd done to us, could he?

For years America had been worried about North Korea getting nukes. Well, it was confirmed during Trump's presidency and things had gotten really tense. Missile tests, insults and threats ramped up the pressure. Kim Jong Un had eventually moderated his tone, and there had been meetings and diplomacy, but things always seemed to be close to boiling point even into the next presidency.

Throw in Putin's Russia making moves in Europe and the threats to the USA seemed clear.

But boy, had they been wrong. While the Pentagon's attention was effectively diverted, the enemy they'd really needed to be concerned about was much more powerful and clever and, even then, working on their plans for expansion. It had suited them perfectly for North Korea and Russia to keep stirring the pot, keeping all the attention off them.

It doesn't really matter anymore, I guess. What happened has happened, and we're the ones left to deal with the consequences.

So again, why waste time thinking about death when it could happen at any second?

Just look at Sarah. She was the first one that Luke and I found. She was a good kid, and only just beginning to come out of the shell she'd retreated into after

'Hell Week.' Dogs got her. A pack had been stalking us for a few miles, they were hungry and mean. I'll never forget her screams. We shot three of them and the rest fled but not before they'd nearly torn her arm clean off...

But I'm getting ahead of myself.

My world changed two years before everyone else's did too. Dad didn't arrive to pick me up from Tommy's at 10am, the arranged time, on the Sunday morning. I called home at 1030 to see where he was, but all I got was the shrill beep, beep, beep of a busy signal. Mr. Benson asked me what my dad's cellphone number was, but I didn't know it.

"I'm sure he won't be much longer," he said, almost managing to mask his annoyance.

Tommy and I went back to his room to play X-Box while we waited. When two hours passed with no word, the Bensons gave me some lunch.

"Tommy and I will drop you home after we eat."

I know it sounds weird, but I kind of knew that something wasn't right. I'd had a strange feeling all that morning, a sense that something bad was going to happen. I didn't know it then, but it had already happened. When Mr. Benson turned onto our street, I knew before I saw them that there would be fire trucks. I don't know how, but I did.

Sure enough, there they were, impossibly red on that bright, sunny, horrible afternoon.

My house was a blackened pile of rubble; the remains of a rotten tooth in the perfect smile of big, neat houses that lined our cul-de-sac.

"Fuck," whispered my friend's dad.

That word coming from the mouth of the conservative Mr. Benson might normally have elicited harsh sniggers from Tommy and me. Not that day. I think I was already in shock, and even Tommy had been stunned into an unusual silence.

Mr. Benson was saying something when we pulled up. I didn't hear what; the rushing sound in my head drowned everything out. I didn't want to open the door. It felt like when I did, I would be opening a door into another existence.

"Isaac, stay there. I'll talk to the police officer." Mr. Benson's words finally cut through the fog in my head.

"It's okay," I said, and pushing past the dread, I opened the door.

Noise assaulted my senses. People yelling, water from firehoses sizzling on smoldering timber, someone crying.

By the mailbox, the one surviving man-made construction on our lot, our beer-bellied neighbor, Bob Johnson, was talking to a police officer. His hair was wild and his face smudged with soot.

"Isaac!" he yelled and rushed over. I took a step back, but he caught me and pulled me into a tight hug. "Thank God you're okay, Isaac!"

He began to sob, his big gut moving up and down against me as his tears wet my cheek. We stood that way for a long time; I didn't know what to say or how to escape his hug. Every time he tried to say something, he broke into sobs again.

Finally, I heard a man's voice over his shoulder.

"Mr. Johnson... please, I'll talk to the boy."

I stumbled a little as the big man let me go. The officer put a steadying hand on my shoulder and guided me to the fence that separated our two properties. That day is still a blur, but I remember looking back at the smoking mess that had been my home before the officer turned me back toward the street. That was worse.

Tommy stood there with his dad's arm around his shoulder, identical looks of pity on their faces and for the first time it hit me that I would never feel my dad's arm around me again. I started to weep as the officer spoke to me.

"I'm so sorry, son. I want you to know that your family wouldn't have felt a thing. It looks like the fire started in the kitchen and they would have been sound asleep. The smoke going through the house meant they didn't wake up or feel pain." He paused, as if unsure how to go on. "Do you have family we can call and get you looked after? Grandparents? Aunts or uncles? Anyone close by?"

I tried to man up, ashamed of my tears. Funny what things seem important to a thirteen-year-old. I shook my head.

"There's no one," I sniveled. "All of my grandparents are dead, and I don't have uncles or aunts."

"It's okay, son, we'll have someone take care of you. Here, come and sit in the patrol car while I make some calls."

The cop turned and headed off to his cruiser. I glanced at the crowd of people that watched from across the street and saw my dad looking right across at me. It was only a second before I realized it wasn't him, just a guy with a beard and similar colored hair. I felt a fresh stab of loss.

That would happen a lot over the next few months. I would be doing something mundane, something where my mind was on auto-pilot, and I would think I saw one of them, Dad or Mom, or Rebecca. At a bus stop. In a supermarket. In a queue at Starbucks. It was a cruel trick of the mind that allowed the reality of my loss to sock me in the guts over and over again.

The cop stopped when he realized I wasn't following and reached for my hand. I absently shook him off and trailed him to his cruiser. He opened the door to the front passenger seat and I climbed in.

I looked around, my boy's curiosity at being in a police car surfacing through the well of grief for a just a moment. I managed to stop crying and wiped my eyes as I listened to the cop make a call back to base. I knew it was about me, but didn't really absorb what was being said.

As he signed off, Tommy's dad approached to the driver's door. He whispered a few words in the officer's ear before passing him a card. The officer nodded and Mr. Benson came around to my side, his face serious. He put a comforting hand on my shoulder.

"Isaac, Tommy and I have to go. I've given the officer my details and told him they can call me anytime and so can you. Take it easy, son. I know it doesn't seem like it now, but everything will be... better in a few weeks." He looked around. "Tommy, come say bye to Isaac."

Tommy looked reluctant as he shuffled forward and offered me his hand. That moment summed up the weirdness of the whole day. We never shook hands; it was always high-fives and laying skin. Still seated, I took his clammy hand awkwardly and shook it.

"See ya, Isaac," my friend mumbled with his eyes down before stepping away.

His dad looked at me one last time, pity in his eyes, before putting his arm around Tommy's shoulders and leading him away. I started to cry again, the familiar faces of my friend and his dad were gone and I was left with strangers. Most of them would have pity in their eyes too, but it was a kind of worn, business-like pity. I might have been the world's newest orphan, but for them, just the latest in a long line.

I never saw Tommy again.

I won't bore you with what happened that afternoon or for the next few weeks, except to say that a social worker got there about an hour after the cop had made his call. Margaret (I don't remember her last name) was about my Mom's age, but with the horned rimmed glasses and dowdy clothes she wore, she looked much older.

She was kind and somehow made me feel better as she drove me to the halfway house. She told me I would stay there until I was placed in a suitable foster home. I'm not going to write about my family's funeral, which happened a week and a half later. It's enough to say that it was the worst day of my life... my old life, anyway.

I was at the halfway house for three weeks before Margaret visited to tell me that a suitable home had been found. I don't remember much of my time there, just the relief of leaving.

I suppose I should have been nervous about meeting new 'parents' but to be honest, I was still kind of numb.

The Pratchetts lived about 30 miles away in a neat brick bungalow. When we were introduced, Mr. and Mrs. Pratchett insisted I call them Randy and Jenny, but as her husband saw Margaret out to her car, Mrs. Pratchett put her arm around me.

"You can call me Mom if you want too," she whispered.

It was insulting and insensitive, even if she was trying to be kind, but I didn't even get angry. At that time, not much seemed to get through.

Randy and Jenny were in their early 30s and didn't have any kids of their own. At first, they seemed okay. They had a nice big house and put me in a huge bedroom with its own flat screen TV, the latest PlayStation, and a computer. Jenny had shown me the room with a flourish, but, with my loss still raw, I wasn't able to do more than say thanks in a flat tone.

I know I was still grieving for my family at that stage, but, from the start, there was something I didn't like about Randy. He seemed too good and wholesome to be true, almost as if he was playing a role in a family movie. Still, it was hard to put my finger exactly on what it was.

One night, about a week after I moved in, he confirmed the bad vibe. I could tell instantly something was not right when I sat down at the table for our evening meal. He stumbled in from the living room. Jenny was unusually quiet and barely looked up from her plate as we began eating. No one had uttered a word when, after a few mouthfuls, Randy placed his fork neatly on the plate and without warning reached over the table and slapped Jenny across the face. Jenny began screaming. No words, just screaming.

I was shocked by the suddenness... the quick violence of it. I sat with my mouth open, my mouthful of mashed potato in danger of spilling out. Then he stood and slapped her again, harder this time, across the other cheek with the back of his hand.

Jenny stopped screaming. She held her face in her hands and began sobbing quietly. I was stunned. I had only ever seen behavior like that on TV. My Mom and Dad had arguments of course, but he had never raised a hand to her.

Randy noticed me staring at him open-mouthed.

"What are you looking at, you little shit?" He yelled at me, flecks of spit flying off his lips.

He glared at me, but I wasn't scared. I think something was (and still is) broken inside me. I stared right back at him, not dropping my gaze from his bloodshot eyes and finished chewing my mashed potato. I guess it freaked him out. Eventually he broke eye contact and called me a foul name under his breath before standing up and kicking over his chair.

I think that was the first time I realized that bullies, no matter how old they are, thrive on fear and if you don't show it, and then have the audacity to stare them down, they back right off... most of the time anyway.

He stalked across to the kitchen counter and snatched up his keys before storming through the door into the hallway. I heard the front door slam a few seconds later, then the sound of his car starting. I put my hand on Jenny's arm.

"It's okay, he's gone. Are you alright?"

My heart went out to her (maybe I wasn't totally numb). Livid marks marred her pale cheeks and her eyes were filled with pain. I'm pretty sure it wasn't just physical pain. She smiled bravely and grasped my hand.

"Look at you, you're twice the man he is and you're only 13. I'm so sorry you had to see that."

"It's okay ..."

We ate the rest of our dinner in silence.

It was back to the halfway house for me the next day. Jenny had called the social worker first thing the next morning.

"Sorry Isaac. I guess I thought having a kid in the house would change him."

I was worried for her but she assured me she would be okay, she was packing her things and leaving Randy as soon as I had gone. She hugged me when I left and I hugged her back just as hard.

"Take care Mrs. Pratchett... Jenny. Thanks for trying."

Margaret, my social worker, was apologetic in the car.

"I'm sorry, Isaac, sometimes, even with all the background checks and interviews we do, the bad ones slip through the cracks."

Nine days later, she took me to meet the Fosters. I didn't have much of a sense of humor at that point or I might have found that funny. Fostered by the Fosters. Unlike the Pratchetts, I liked them both straight away.

They were older than Randy and Jenny and had been fostering kids for a long time. Their last foster son had just turned 19 and left for college a month before. They had an empty house and were ready to take on a new kid that needed a break. That kid happened to be me.

I have to admit that as time went by, my numbness turned to resentment, resentment at the world for taking my parents away. It shames me now, but some of that angst was taken out on the Fosters.

I'd act out and get into trouble at home and at school. To their credit, they always accepted the place I was in and worked hard to make sure I knew that they'd be there for me. Slowly I started to come around and, by the end (literally the end), we were getting along really well, so much so that I was almost beginning to think that I had a found a new place to belong.

Alan Foster was a retired postal worker, and despite any rumors or jokes that you may have heard about postal workers and their anger issues, let me tell you,

Alan was one of the most mild and patient men that I've ever met.

He was silver-haired and soft spoken, and what I remember best about him was his quiet strength. Eleanor had been the stay-at-home mom for those before me and had a patience and calmness that complemented Alan. Sometimes I wonder if it hurt her, how few of us ever actually called her by that title: 'mom'. I know I never did, not when she could hear me, at least.

I spent over a year and a half with the Fosters in a town called Fort Carter. I started at Fort Carter Junior High while I was still dealing with the death of my parents and the hole that their loss had created inside of me. I had few friends at school.

I pretty much kept to myself in the lunchroom and during breaks, and rarely spoke up in class unless I was called upon. The other kids thought I was weird and, to tell you the truth, I think most of the teachers did too. I ended up spending a lot of time in the school counselor's office. Mr. Jennings tried to break into my shell and I resisted with all of my might. I had to admire his tenacity though; I think he wanted to help me just as much as the Fosters did.

One of the few joys in my life was Kung Fu. I took it up at Alan's insistence and it was the best thing I could have done. I took to it like a toddler to ice cream and before long I was going three nights a week. I attained my black belt within a year and even competed in the Rhode Island State Championships.

Not only was it a good physical outlet for me, I look back now and see how much it did for my mental discipline too.

All in all, things were good and getting better.

It was the middle of October when I recall first hearing that something was amiss. I had helped Eleanor clear up the supper dishes and wandered into the living room where Alan watched the news each evening. As I did so, I noticed a banner across the bottom of the screen alerting the viewers of a special report.

"... and now some breaking news out of North Korea," Sarah Mulligan, the Channel Seven news co-anchor was saying. "Tom?"

"We are getting reports of a flu-like disease that is sweeping the nation of North Korea," Tom Dallard said, taking over from his on-air partner. "Preliminary reports suggest that as many as one million Koreans in the Pyongyang region have fallen ill with this mystery virus over the last few days. The North Korean government has closed their borders even tighter than they normally are and their leader has not been seen in public in over 48 hours. Their government news agency has remained silent on the issue of the disease. Experts here in the US believe that casualties could be in the thousands," he paused, looking at his notes and then off to one side before looking back to the camera.

"We now take you live to a statement being given by Lloyd Ackerman, Chief of Public Relations for the Center for Disease Control."

"Doesn't look good," muttered Alan, as we watched the camera cut away to a shot of a tall man standing behind a podium bearing the circular CDC emblem. I focused in on what Dr. Ackerman was saying.

"... isolationist policies make it hard for us to get accurate, real-time information on this outbreak; at the same time, those policies seem to be containing the outbreak to North Korea itself. At this point, all we know is the disease appears to be a fast acting form of influenza. Symptoms develop rapidly after exposure and, in many cases, fatality occurs within a few days. Again, because of the nature of dealing with information from North Korea, we do not know the exact fatality percentages or the rate of infection. At this time, we are coordinating with the FAA and the Department of Homeland Security to ensure everybody flying into the United States from East Asia will be quarantined for 24 hours after arrival to ensure that symptoms do not develop. We do not think there is a clear and present danger to the people of the United States at this time, but, when dealing with a disease such as this, the situation is always fluid and can change at any time. I'll now take a few questions from the press." He pointed to a reporter in the crowd in front of him.

"How bad is this going to get, Doctor?"

"Well, it certainly seems that there is a real mystery to this one. Flu season in South-East Asia had been relatively good this year, so it is worrying that it seemed to come out of the blue, hard and fast," Ackerman replied. "Whether it turns out to be something less dangerous than originally thought, like the infamous Swine Flu, is unknowable at this time. While that outcome is something we can all hope for, I think it would be wise to look at this as if it were the worst case scenario until proven otherwise... and, if that is the case, then yes, it is going to be bad. Possibly very bad.

"Based on some of the reports coming out of North Korea, we could be looking at something as virulent as the Spanish influenza. But, as I said, that is pure conjecture at this time."

He motioned to another reporter, but Alan switched off the television before the question came.

I often wondered later if Dr. Ackerman lived long enough to realize just how much his 'worst case scenario' had underestimated the flu that was, unbeknown to the rest of the world, decimating the North Korean adult population.

"Do you have any homework, Isaac?" Alan asked from his recliner.

"No, sir," I replied. It was a lie, but a small one. I actually had a dozen math problems I needed to do for my algebra class, but I my class in the afternoon and figured I'd just do them at lunch the next day. It's not like I had any friends to hang out with during lunch time.

The next day the 'Pyongyang flu,' as it had been dubbed, was the talk of the school. According to the loose teenage gossip it was going to spread and result in the end of the world.

Bernie Bova, my lab partner in Physical Science, wouldn't shut up about how it was a government conspiracy, and that President Riley had finally had enough of Kim Jong-Un, his bad haircut and his constant threats of nuclear war.

"Telling you man, its biological warfare. We're taking those bitches down!"

At the time, none of us knew how close to the truth he actually was, although he got the source of the attack wrong. That sort of talk went on for a few days, while news stories lingered on the evening news and in the papers, but then, like all news stories without a direct effect on the majority of Americans, they petered off, aided by the fact that the North Korean government had virtually sealed off their country, not only the borders but also all telecommunication, media, and internet.

Within a couple of weeks there was nothing besides the occasional mention, regularly recycled stories and speculation on the 24 hour news channels. Going about my daily life, I heard no news about the Pyongyang flu for nearly two whole weeks.

Then on Halloween day, the Chinese government announced that they were sending an expeditionary taskforce over the border into North Korea. Communications from the North Korean government had by then ceased and the American military had announced that their satellites were currently detecting little or no evidence of life. This essentially meant no movement of vehicles or transport, no communications, and little evidence of population in over two weeks.

With this deafening silence hanging over North Korea, the Chinese had the support of the United Nations. Even our government, long critical of China's inaction when it came to North Korea, but also wary of their expansion in the Pacific, approved. Everybody wanted to know what had transpired there.

Halloween didn't really mean a lot to me. I had never been much into candy, and at nearly 15-years old, I felt that I was a little bit too old for trick-or-treating even though Eleanor tried to talk me into it. I refused, politely of course, and spent the evening watching CNN's live updates of the Chinese expedition with Alan.

The Chinese government was very forthcoming with what they were finding, releasing video footage to their own and Western news outlets but drawing the line at a live feed.

I had to suppress shudders watching the recorded video footage from the helmet cams of the Chinese soldiers. They were marching through a wasteland. Something like 96 percent of the adult population had succumbed to the infection; children appeared to be unaffected but the reports showed them being rounded up by soldiers and transported to camps where the Chinese government assured the world they would be cared for until a long term solution could be found. No one in the scientific community could explain why children seemed to be immune to the infection, although there was some wild speculation.

While they were physically unaffected by the flu, being left to their own devices, alone and unsupervised, had not been kind to them. The first groups of children filmed seemed wild, almost feral and I remember wondering how they could have fallen so far in such a short period of time. Watching them, some snarling and spitting at the soldiers, others staring dumbly,

I was reminded of Lord of the Flies. The novel by William Golding is about a group of kids shipwrecked on an island with no adults. Left to their own devices, with little chance of rescue, the children's descent into savagery had been quick and not at all pretty. Perhaps Golding's fiction was pretty close to the mark?

Within a day or so, the Chinese government's willingness to share information dried up. They occupied North Korea with a sizeable force and declared it a quarantine zone. Their president, only in the job for less than year and known for his aggressive politics, assured the world that their scientists were hard at work studying the disease and would reveal their findings when the study was complete.

Needless to say, a diplomatic crisis ensued, neither South Korea nor the US was happy with China's forces crossing into North Korea and the president ordered our Pacific fleet into international waters off the coast of South Korea.

For a few more days, the Pyongyang flu and devastation of North Korea along with the huffing and puffing and possibility of war was on everybody's minds, but eventually it slowly faded once more. Deals were done, and China agreed to allow UN forces on the ground in NK. The normal reactions to a horrendous human disaster played out; celebrities cried on TV and criticized the president for not offering more money, politicians pledged to push through relief packages and the conspiracy theorists threw their unsubstantiated theories around with wild abandon. Again, as the news cycle churned and it stopped being front and center, the celebrities and politicians moved on to their next pet cause and North Korea and the Pyongyang flu faded from most people's minds.

Nobody seriously suspected then that the Pyongyang flu was anything more than a terrible pandemic that science would soon tame, as it had done many times before. The fact was, besides the conspiracy theorists, nobody was even close to the truth: that the infection of North Korea was a trial, a dry run for the real deal. NK's isolationist policies had made it the perfect petri dish and, soon enough, the results of that experiment would be used to irrevocably swing the balance of power in the world.

2

Three days later I was in a dark mood as I sat in the school office during third period. It was my 15th birthday, but I wasn't really in the mood to celebrate. I had my head bowed and was doing my best to ignore the world around me.

I was thinking about my parents and sister and the last birthday I had shared with them. It had seemed nothing special then, just my favorite home-cooked meal and a simple chocolate cake, but now it was a precious memory. Funny how some things become more significant later on.

My thoughts drifted to the North Korean children and how millions of them had also had their parents ripped from them. The world was a shitty place.

I was faintly aware of somebody sitting down in the seat next to me, but kept my head buried in my hands. I didn't feel up to making conversation.

"So, whatcha here for?"

I sighed. Some people just can't read body language. I thought about ignoring the question, but in the end I sat back in my chair and looked up to see a tall, red-headed boy slouched in the plastic chair next to mine. I knew him, of course. Luke Merritt was my age and one of the more popular kids in my class, his outgoing personality more than making up for his freckles and gangly appearance.

"Don't know," I said with a shrug. "I got a note to come see Mr. Jennings. How about you?"

"I'm here to see Dan the Man," he said, referring to Vice Principal Dan Haralson. 'Dan the Man' was his nickname amongst the student body, earned by his easy-going, 'cool' attitude toward the kids.

"Tyler Lane was bugging Sheri Denison in PE, and when he grabbed her boob, I felt I just had to step in, you know? I mean, they're so perfect that no one with the IQ of a brick should ever be able to touch them ... ever! Anyway, one swift kick to the nards later and here I am. Still, I'd rather be here waiting to see the Man than sitting with my swollen balls on ice at the nurse's station."

He was clearly pleased with himself and despite my mood I found myself smiling.

"You know, Haralson's going to give you detention at the very least. I know he's pretty cool and all, but he's tough on fighting," I said. "He might even suspend you."

"Totally worth it, man," Luke replied. "A suspension isn't going to stop me from helping out someone in trouble. Besides, have you seen Sheri? Maybe she'll want to thank me in person some time."

He nudged me with his elbow and winked and I smiled again.

Begrudgingly, I felt myself begin to like Luke. It was hard not to. We might have talked more, but just then

Mr. Jennings opened his door and called me into his office.

I felt my smile melt away.

"Seeya Isaac," Luke said.

I gave a half-wave but didn't smile as I followed the school counselor into his office. I know now my aloofness was a defense mechanism, something I put in place to be sure I could never get close to anyone again, but I didn't know another way to handle my situation.

Jennings' office was small and cramped. A desk and two metal bookshelves dominated the room and, when the coat rack was taken into account, the only place for a visitor was on the hard plastic chair set in front of the desk.

"Have a seat, Isaac," Mr. Jennings said, dropping into the black cushioned chair behind his desk. "Miss Babette mentioned that you've been even more distant in class the last couple of days, so I thought I'd have a chat with you and see if you're okay."

I looked around the office, as I often did when called there. My eyes finally came to rest on a poster for an old movie that Mr. Jennings had on the wall above his head. I have never seen 'Rosencrantz & Guildenstern Are Dead' but I always thought I'd be interested to watch it and work out if there was a reason he had that particular poster on his wall. Maybe there was no deep reason? Maybe he just liked the movie.

"Well, Isaac?"

I looked back down at him.

"No, sir, nothing out of the ordinary," I replied. There was no way I was going to mention it was my birthday. "I guess I've just been thinking about those poor kids in North Korea a lot this week is all. How they lost everyone."

"At least they are still alive," Mr. Jennings said. "So they're lucky in that regard at least."

I felt a flame of anger lick at my detachment.

"Are they?" I asked in a tight voice.

"Well, maybe not," he said, apparently realizing he'd put his foot in it. "I didn't mean to be callous. Of course, you're right, nothing would be worse than losing parents at a young age."

I swallowed my anger and zoned out again.

3

The rest of the year passed without incident until school let out for winter break. Leaving Fort Carter Junior High the Friday before Christmas, I had no way of knowing that I'd never set foot in the school again. My time in a classroom was over, but it was not the end of my lessons.

When it happened, it happened fast. The United States of America, the greatest nation on earth, functionally ceased to exist in less than a week. The first people started getting sick on Christmas Day.

"Thanks, Alan, Eleanor, I love it!" I said, holding the small drone I'd just unwrapped in my hands. I felt happy, part of a real family for the first time since the fire. Most of the presents that they had given me were sensible – a sweater, some woolen socks, a new backpack to carry my school books in, but the remote-controlled drone was the first real present I had gotten since my parents died.

I attempted to fly the mini-drone around the living room, but it was difficult to control and many crash landings and retrievals followed while I got used to it. Finally, I got the hang of it and followed it as I guided it on its most successful flight through the dining room and into the kitchen - where it promptly crashed into a wall above Eleanor's China cabinet, two of its rotors flying in different directions as it spun on the floor like a dying fly.

The thought of playing had been absent from my mind for over a year and for just a brief moment, as we fell about laughing (all except Eleanor who was horrified at the damage I could have done to her good China) at my ineptness as a pilot, I felt almost like a normal kid again.

"Are you all right, Al?" Eleanor was saying to her husband as I re-entered the dining room after putting the blades back on. "You've been coughing an awful lot this morning."

"Just a bit of a tickle in the back of my throat," he said. "I'll be fine."

"Judith said there was a bug going around," Eleanor said, shaking her head. "Let me get you some warm salt water to gargle; perhaps we can knock it out of you before it really sets up shop."

"I hope so. I took a mega-dose of vitamin C this morning when I first noticed it," Alan said. "You know how I hate being sick."

"Doesn't everybody hate being sick?" I asked earnestly.

Alan smiled.

"That they do, Son."

"Isaac, can you clean up the wrapping paper and put your gifts away?" Eleanor asked, before heading to the kitchen to fetch the salt water for Alan. "John and Amy should be here soon."

John and Amy were two of the kids they had fostered before me. John was in college now, down in Providence, and Amy was living up in Boston. Both still had strong feelings for the Fosters though, and came to visit often on holidays. Amy even called them Mom and Dad. I had met both a few times before and they seemed like good people, just the sort of kids you'd expect to come out of a family life crafted by Alan and Eleanor.

I gathered up my gifts and took them to my room, where I dumped them in a pile on the bed. I had to admit to myself that I was looking forward to Christmas dinner. With John and Amy there it would be almost like the family gatherings I fondly remembered from before my grandparents had died, just a few years before my parents.

When I went back to the living room to gather up the torn wrapping paper, Eleanor was on the kitchen phone.

"Oh, I'm so sorry to hear that, dear. I hope you feel better soon ... No, no, don't worry about it, perhaps you can get up to visit before New Year's. I'm sure he'll understand ... Get some rest and eat some soup; chikken noodle helps your body get over bugs. Love you, too. Bye, John."

Eleanor looked tired as she put the phone down, but when she noticed me, she perked up. I knew it was just a front.

"That was John," she said. "He's feeling a bit under the weather and won't make it tonight. Amy texted my cell phone a half-hour ago though, and she should be here any minute."

I felt a small loss now that John wouldn't be coming. I really liked him. From the little pieces of information that the Fosters had given me, I knew his struggles had been far rougher than mine before he had come to live with them. That he'd turned out to be such a good, well-adjusted person and had the opportunity to go to college was a testament to the Fosters.

I went and looked through the dining room window after I'd finished cleaning up the wreckage of the unwrapping. Snow had started to fall. It was the first snowfall of the year and the weatherman had not predicted it.

It looked like there was going to be a white Christmas in Fort Carter, Rhode Island after all.

I dutifully lowered my head and clasped my hands as Alan said grace. At that time in my life I was angry with God, but not completely ready to give up on the idea of his existence. The meal had been prepared with expectations that John would be there as well, so there was more than enough food to go around – ham, cornbread stuffing, mashed potatoes and gravy, green bean casserole, pumpkin and apple pies for dessert. It was a veritable feast. Given the things I've eaten just to stay alive in the weeks since that day, I almost feel bad about taking that meal for granted.

The conversation around the dinner table was merry, with Alan, Eleanor, and Amy all laughing and reminiscing about the past. At one point during the meal, my mood had taken a turn for the worse. Rather than making me feel better, being reminded of the family gatherings that I remembered so fondly actually made me feel down. Amy glanced over at me.

"Why don't you show me the presents you got after dinner?" she said, putting her hand on mine. "Mom said that you got a drone! I'm jealous, they never got me anything so cool."

I shrugged.

"It's just a toy."

Amy was nice enough, but she was older than John, in her mid-20s, and always seemed more like a visiting adult than a potential sibling. I ate a few more bites but found that the food had begun to lose its taste. I could tell that one of my mopey moods (that's what Eleanor called them) was about to hit me hard. These bouts of unhappiness were less frequent since I had been living with the Fosters, but I had not completely left them behind.

"May I be excused?" I asked, looking up at Alan.

"Sure, take your plate to the kitchen," Alan said. "Don't let yourself get too down in the dumps though, mister. Later this evening we are going to go caroling around the neighborhood."

"Okay."

I got up and picked up my plate.

"Is he still depressed?" Amy asked quietly as I went into the kitchen.

I heard the question, but not the reply.

We never did go caroling that night. When the time came, Alan was feeling much worse than he had been that morning and had developed a fever to go with his sore throat and cough. Amy said she was beginning to feel sick too.

Before she left, she came up to my room to look over my presents and chat in an attempt to cheer me up. It was nice of her and I appreciated it, but it was an awkward, stilted conversation.

"You look terrible," I said with typical teenage bluntness, during a particularly long pause.

She really did. There were dark circles under her eyes that hadn't been there just two hours ago and every few minutes she coughed into her handkerchief. I remember being amazed how she had gone from being perfectly healthy to obviously ill so quickly. Her hand fluttered to her throat.

"Yes, I think I better get going."

I held my breath as she gave me a hug and left.

4

An urgent rapping on my bedroom door woke me the next morning. The clock on my bedside table read 5:58. I sat up, as another series of heavier raps cut through the sleep fog in my head.

"Isaac!"

"Yeah?"

"Isaac, Alan isn't doing well this morning. I am going to drive him over to United General," Eleanor called through the door. "Are you going to be alright here by yourself for a while?"

"Yeah, sure," I replied, managing to keep the annoyance out of my voice. I was certainly old enough to look after myself in an empty house.

I thought about jumping up to go with them, but by the time I had decided to act on those thoughts I heard the car start up and back down the driveway. I got up anyway and wandered through the empty house. Some leftover ham and mashed potatoes provided a decent enough breakfast and I soon wandered into the living room to turn on the television. The channel it was tuned to was broadcasting a news report, so I switched it to another station, only to see more news. In fact most stations were broadcasting breaking news.

This must be big, I thought, and settled onto the sofa, remote in hand.

I saw the familiar podium with the CDC emblem, and there was Dr. Ackerman walking up to it again. At first, I thought that they might be replaying the press conference from before Halloween, but I realized this was new as soon as Ackerman started talking.

My breakfast felt heavy in my stomach as I listened intently.

"It has been confirmed that the infection known as the Pyongyang flu is currently sweeping the Eastern seaboard of the United States." As he spoke, his face was as emotionless as a stone slab. "At this point it appears that the disease only affects those people approximately 17-years old and up. Or, to be more exact, people who have passed the growth stage where both the distal end of the humerus and the distal end of the tibia are fully fused. This generally happens between the ages of 15 and 17. We still don't know why this is."

"What about adults?" one of the reporters shouted, briefly interrupting the press conference.

"Adults exposed to the virus have a high probability of contracting the disease. This seems to vary across phenotype or race, but, at this juncture, it is impossible to say whether people such as Native Americans are truly immune to the disease, or if it simply takes longer for them to succumb." Ackerman held up his hands to quiet the growing murmuring among the reporters. "It is not my intention to cause a panic here. The CDC is getting ahead of this thing, and we should have the outbreak under control within a matter of days. The first case was reported yesterday, but not confirmed as Pyongyang flu until this morning. From what we can tell so far, it spreads like a normal flu virus, so wash your hands, cover your mouth and nose when coughing and sneezing and stay away from crowded areas as much as possible..."

A man in a rumpled suit rushed up to the podium from off-camera, whispered something in Ackerman's ear and passed him a sheet of paper. The CDC publicist's face drained of all color as he read the words before screwing the paper up into a tight ball.

"What is it? What's happening?" the same reporter from before called.

"CDC scientists have just confirmed that H3J2, the virus commonly known as the Pyongyang flu, is, in fact, a man-made biological," Ackerman said.

I fancied that he had the same look on his face as mine when I had seen the smoking ruins of my home from the backseat of Mr. Benson's car.

"It appears to be airborne. At this time, the latest estimates are that up to 90 percent of the population of the East coast is suffering from infection, and the infection ... the weaponized virus ... seems to be moving westward at a rate of over one hundred miles per hour. At this rate, every part of the continental United States… in fact the entire continent of North America, will be affected within the next 24 hours. The CIA isn't yet calling this a terrorist attack, but, and this is purely speculation on my part, all signs are pointing that way."

All hell broke loose in the conference room. The microphone caught the sound of women and men crying as dozens of reporters rushed for the exits. The more hardened veterans clamored closer to Dr. Ackerman yelling more questions, while to the left of the podium I noticed the man who had delivered the awful message coughing into his hand.

Ackerman only answered one more question, a high pitched and panicked, "What do we do?"

"Stay in your homes ... and pray to God ..."

I switched off the television and went to the kitchen. Picking up the phone, I dialed Eleanor's cell number and waited impatiently as it went through to her voice mail.

"Eleanor, I just saw on the news that the Pyongyang flu has been released here ... they are saying that terrorists are spreading it around or something. Are you and Alan okay?" I managed to stammer out before the phone beeped again, ending the voice mail.

Not sure what else to do, I hung up and then immediately dialed the number for Margaret, the social worker who had placed me with the Fosters. Once again, it rang out and I got a message saying that she would be out of the office until January 2nd. Hanging up the phone, I went back to the fridge to cut off a bit more ham. I felt lost and alone. All I could think about was the grainy video of the feral children in North Korea.

Eleanor and Alan returned in the early afternoon. She had not been able to get him in to see a doctor at all. The Emergency Room had been swamped long before their arrival. I helped her move Alan, by this point weak and delirious with fever, to their bedroom, where she laid him down and covered him with a bed sheet.

"Run to the freezer and bring me the ice pack," Eleanor said. "I'm worried that he's getting too hot." When I returned with the ice pack, she put it in a pillowcase and placed it on Alan's forehead.

"Oh, Alan, please don't leave me," she whispered, and kissed his brow tenderly.

We sat by his side for a while and then, after he'd fallen into a fitful sleep, went to the living room to watch the news. If anything, the situation had gotten even more horrific since I had turned it off that morning. We learned that the Chinese government was now admitting responsibility for the attack and claiming all of North America by right of conquest.

Not terror then. War.

The other nations of the world were protesting loudly, but the threat to them was implicit and they appeared afraid to make any real moves to help America for fear of the H3J2 virus being turned on them, as well.

Watching the sniffling and coughing reporters, we did learn a bit about the virus though. The disease affected nearly all adults exposed except for - it was rumored - those who were of ethnic Chinese origin. Its fatality rate was a staggering 96 percent. Those few that did survive were generally left as vegetables, with permanent brain damage as a result of the prolonged, high fever that was associated with the infection.

It seemed that the body could produce a previously unknown antibody to fight the disease, but it only did so from a few specific locations, all of them yet to be fused areas of bones such as the tibia and the humerus.

By about age 16 though, those areas had fused, and the body became incapable of producing the specific antibodies, ironically dubbed the 'Funny antibody'.

Those under 16 or 17 exposed to the virus had the antibodies and would be forever immune to the virus. Those who did not, faced almost certain death. The professionalism and bravery of the reporters, reporting while sick, knowing that they were most likely going to be dead within the next few hours, left an indescribable impression on me. I plan to fight with every last ounce of my being to stay alive, but I sincerely hope that if the time comes and, I will face death with as much courage as those reporters did during Hell Week.

5

Alan died around midnight.

Eleanor lay down with him on their bed, her head on his shoulder while she cried. I hugged them both and then stood and watched helplessly for a few minutes before going to my room. I sat on my bed with my arms wrapped tightly around my knees as I listened to her sobbing through the walls.

It was happening again. I had finally started to feel like I belonged and now my new family was being torn away from me just as surely as my real family had been. If anything, this was more painful because it was happening slowly and even though I knew it was happening, I was powerless to stop it. Eleanor was sick too. She was trying to hide it, but I knew that within a day, two at most, I was going to be alone again.

An hour and a half later, the sobbing stopped. At first, I thought she'd fallen asleep but then I heard rustling in their closet. It backed onto the wall of my room, so I could hear quite clearly as she rummaged around. Actually, it was less like rummaging and more like she was tearing the closet apart. I wondered what she was hunting for. Then the sounds stopped.

Several minutes passed and believe it or not, in my sitting position I began to doze off.

BOOM!

I jumped, startled by the bang. When I realized what it meant, I wrapped my arms tighter around my legs.

The house fell into a deep silence as I sat with tears running down my face.

At some point I lay down, pulling blankets over me. I slept deeply and dreamlessly until the morning light was shining through my window. I finally got up the courage to go into their bedroom, knowing with the same certainty that I had known about the fire trucks almost two years earlier, what I would find.

Eleanor was slumped across Alan's body. There was a red mist-like spray on the walls and headboard of the bed and Eleanor's arm dangled off the mattress, limp and lifeless. Near her open hand, on the floor, there was a short barreled revolver.

I knew what she had done, but my mind refused to accept it.

"Eleanor?" I asked, stepping forward into the room. "Eleanor ... Mom?"

There was no movement. Then, moving closer, I saw the neat, perfectly round hole in her temple. A small amount of blood had leaked out of it and down the side of her neck, matting her shoulder length hair in a dark clump. I didn't go any closer.

I tried calling 9-1-1, of course, but I was greeted with a disconnected message. There was no signal at all on Eleanor's cell so I used the land line to try calling John and Amy several times each. There was a dial tone, but only empty air after I dialed their cell numbers.

I put on my coat and went next door to the Moorcock house; they had always seemed like good neighbors and I knew they would help if they were in any state. Nobody answered the door. Crunching back across the snow-covered lawn I looked up and down our street. There was no movement at all and, despite looking like a winter wonderland, the familiar neighborhood landscape felt sinister and full of secrets. I picked up my pace and bolted the front door once I was back inside.

I decided I would just have to close Alan and Eleanor up in their bedroom for the time being and deal with them later. After shutting their door I headed into the kitchen, pondering my situation.

There was plenty of food left over from Christmas dinner and in the pantry, and the gas and electricity were still on too. The rarely used fireplace had a good stock of kindling and logs, and altogether, I guessed I could last a good month if I had too. Surely the authorities would get a handle on this disaster in that time?

The TV channels started going off the air that afternoon, with most of them completely off air by New Year's Eve. There were no fireworks that day. No big ball dropped in New York City. No one celebrated the turning of an era. America had fallen.

It was a lonely few days. I read books. I tried the phone hundreds of times. I slept a lot and ate a lot more than I would normally through sheer boredom.

It was on January 1st when the last news channel still on air reported that the Chinese army had begun landing on American soil. The Chinese government broadcast statements on radio and TV, welcoming the children of America as citizens of New China and promising re-education and adoption into the new world order but Tom Dallard, the last news anchor doing live broadcasts from his station in Boston, told of Chinese soldiers rounding up the children of New York and Baltimore and other major cities and forming them into work gangs to clear bodies. He backed up these claims with a snippet of cellphone footage smuggled into his TV station.

It was apparent that we were to be nothing but slaves to these new overlords.

Dallard was one of those few non-Chinese people who seemed immune to the infection. Whether that was because of a genetic defect or because he had been exposed to a similar enough pathogen when he was younger, he was one of the 4 percent.

He kept on reporting to the last and on January 2nd, alone in an empty studio, talking to the one camera that was focused on him, he spoke stoically over loud banging and the sound of breaking glass. It was distant but getting closer every second.

"... and so America ... children of America, time is running out for me, but know this. America is still the home of the brave and it can again be the land of the free. Where you can, band together, find places to hide from the invaders and live to fight another day. Avenge your parents any way that you can ... look out for each other."

There was an even louder crash and Dallard flinched, somehow looking noble and brave even with the uncharacteristic three day growth and rumpled, unwashed clothes he wore.

"This is Tom Dallard, sign-"

I sat there with my heart beating hard in my chest as two Chinese soldiers tackled Dallard from his chair before he could complete his sign off. One hit him viciously over the head with his rifle butt and then they bent over and dragged his unconscious figure out of view. For the second time in a few days I heard a loud gunshot, this one signifying the end of the America I had known.

I sat staring at the screen for a long time, feeling sick to my stomach. Tom Dallard, in my mind, was the last great American hero, and he deserves to be remembered with the rest of them.

6

January 4th, two days after the live broadcast death of Tom Dallard, was the day I realized I was going to have to fight to survive, and to perhaps do things that no 15-year old kid ... no kid at all ... should have to do.

That was the day looters came to my neighborhood. It had been at least a week since I had seen anybody in our street – not really surprising considering most of the people living there had been around the same age as the Fosters, their children already grown and gone.

I was flicking through the channels on the television trying to find anything at all when I heard the rumble of a car engine. I ran to the window and peered through a crack in the blinds.

A red Toyota pickup truck was cruising slowly down the street, its exhaust pluming in the cold winter air. Excited to see someone – *anyone* – alive, I nearly ran right out to wave them down. Something, a feeling maybe, stopped me and I decided to watch them through the blinds instead.

It slowly cruised right to the end of the street and turned the corner. I was suddenly regretful. Maybe they were looking for survivors? Just people trying to help? I had to find out. I quickly grabbed my coat, pulled on my shoes and ran for the front door, my heart beating hard.

As I grasped the door handle, I heard the rumble again. They had gone around the block and were coming my direction again and it sounded like they were driving more slowly than before. Again, I decided against running out to wave them down and went back to my position at the window.

Within a few seconds they came into view and then stopped in front of Judge Petersen's house; it was across the street and two houses down. The doors opened and three people got out, one was a man with greyish hair, the others looked to be teenagers, one about my age and the other as big as the man. The man stopped just after getting out of the driver's door to lean across the hood, coughing. As he straightened up, I was shocked to see he had a long gun in his hands. As I watched, the teens reached into the cab of the pickup and took out more guns.

I didn't know that much about guns then, everything I knew about them came from television and movies, but I recognized that the two younger figures carried double barreled shotguns and the one held by the coughing man was a rifle.

From my vantage point behind the blinds, I saw the man wave toward the Petersen house, directing the teenagers to the front door. The boy tried the handle and when he found it locked, he stepped aside for the man, who busted it open with one strong kick. They disappeared inside.

Maybe five minutes later they emerged, each carrying a large black garbage bag filled, I assume, with whatever they had looted from Petersen's home. They trotted back to the pickup and dropped the bags in the bed.

The sick man then pointed to the house next door to the Petersen residence and the teenagers disappeared inside.

A sliver of fear shot through me – what if they came to my house? I didn't know what they were looking for, money, jewelry, or just food and supplies, but given the fact that they were armed, I was more concerned about what they might do if they found me here.

Just as worrying was the idea that if I managed to hide and they didn't find me, what would I do if they took all the food? One thing I knew for certain, I'd have a better chance against armed men if I was armed myself, so with gritted teeth I left the window and ran to Alan and Eleanor's bedroom.

It had been a week, and the smell of spoiling meat hit me as soon as I opened the door. I tried not to look at the bodies of my foster parents as I paused at the threshold of the darkened room. To say I was creeped out would be sugarcoating it and, for a second, I almost turned around, armed looters or no armed looters.

In the end, I took a deep breath and crossed the room. Still averting my gaze from them, I bent and reached out for shape of the revolver on the floor. That was when my elbow bumped the bed and Eleanor's cold, stiff hand fell onto mine. The shriek that escaped my throat would have been right at home in a horror movie. I snatched up the weapon and jumped away from the bed and stopped, my heart hammering painfully in my chest.

I was about to leave when my eyes fell upon the open gun case sitting on the dresser. It was lined with foam cut out in the shape of the gun and had another rectangular cut out which contained a box marked *Remington .38 SPECIAL*.

I pulled out the box and opened it. It was full of extra bullets. Grateful, I slipped it under my coat and into the pocket of my gray hooded sweatshirt before heading out and back to the front window.

Although it had seemed like an eternity, my trip to the Fosters' bedroom had been brief enough that the two teenagers had not yet returned to the truck from the second home. I watched the driver. He was now slumped against the front fender of the pickup, his hacking cough clearly audible to me. I wondered vaguely how much longer he'd last, certainly not more than another day but then he must have been tough to last this long.

I know it might seem horrible, me thinking about the life of another person in such an abstract way, with no real sense of pity, but survivors adapt and one of the first things that seems to go is compassion. I think the previous couple of years had already stunted my empathy toward my fellow human beings, so maybe I already had a leg up on the other survivors.

A minute after I returned to the window, the looters returned to the truck and dumped their goods. Almost in slow motion I saw the man point in my direction.

Not *at* me, of course, but at my home. The older teen, perhaps only a few years older than me, maybe 16 or 17, but large for his age gestured to the younger guy and they crossed the road and started across the snowy lawn towards my front door. Time was up.

7

I dug under my coat and pulled out the gun. Now I was committed to using it, the weapon seemed heavier; I was reminded of Frodo's ring approaching Mordor. With shaking hands I stuck the barrel through the blinds and the cold steel muzzle chattered against the glass pane.

I think they saw me at the last second, but it didn't matter. I pulled the trigger. The handgun bucked in my hands, the report far louder than I had expected but the bullet made nothing more than a jagged little hole as it passed through the glass.

The man leaning against the fender jerked and grabbed at his thigh, his scream of agony cutting like a laser through the ringing in my ears. I hadn't been aiming at him. I hadn't been aiming at anything in particular, I just wanted to scare them off but my round had found him anyway.

He was sliding down onto the road holding his leg when everything exploded.

The window detonated, the blast ripping through the wooden blinds. The blinds themselves protected me from the majority of the flying glass and the shotgun pellets had struck about a foot to my right. I fell to my knees and scrambled behind the sofa.

Another shot blew the blinds completely off the window and they clattered onto the floor. I thought about going back to the window and shooting back, but I was clearly outgunned. They didn't know that though, and I realized my best chance of survival was for them to give up, precisely because they didn't know what awaited them inside.

If not I would put a bullet in the first one through the door. I slithered along the floor in front of the sofa until I could see the front door through the opening into the hallway.

I lay there watching the front door with the gun at the ready for what may have been a minute when it dawned on me that they might circle around the house and come in the back. *Shit!*

I was about to get up when I heard the man I shot scream to his partners in crime.

"Forget it! Get me home you eejits!"

I held my breath until I heard the truck start up. Keeping low, I crawled across the room to the second window and, half expecting to find myself looking down the barrel of a gun, I parted the blinds and peeked through.

The wounded man had been loaded into the bed of the pickup and was sitting with his back to the rear wall of the cab, his face a rictus of agony as the younger boy climbed in. He had barely settled when the pickup, now driven by the older boy, took off with a squeal of tires.

Luckily for me, they had cut their losses and run. I let out a long sigh.

The encounter prompted me to take stock of my situation. I had probably a week's worth of canned goods left. The milk, eggs, and other perishables from the refrigerator were gone, all except for half a bottle of Eleanor's prune juice. I had never touched the stuff and didn't plan on starting now, no matter how thirsty I got.

There was also a six-pack of beer Alan had bought to share with John on Christmas Day. I stayed away from the beer too, not because I had any aversion to alcohol or anything, but I wasn't a huge fan of the taste. In any case, my mind needed to stay sharp and alert in case more looters came.

The danger presented by the looters had given me quite a wakeup call. So, after a meal of canned baked beans, I did a Karate workout, running through my old sparring drills and doing push-ups and sit ups. While I worked out, I thought about the prospect of the looters returning for revenge, perhaps a bigger danger than my dwindling supplies.

I seriously considered packing up what I could in the Fosters' car and driving away right then. Two things stopped me. First was lack of a clear destination; where would I go? I had some vague notion of going to Canada. Even though I had seen some reports that the flu had spread there, I didn't think they were the real target of the Chinese, just collateral damage.

Second – I didn't really know how to drive.

The power went out sometime before dawn the next morning and the decision was made for me. Whether or not I could drive or had a place to go, it was clear I couldn't stay where I was.

I found the keys to Eleanor's car in her purse on the kitchen counter and gathered some warm clothes, a couple of blankets and what food I had left and loaded it into the back seat of her Honda Accord. I opened the garage door, lucky it was not powered, and started her car. Again, lucky it was an auto. I let it run as I went inside to grab the gun and ammo.

On the way out I stopped by the Foster's bedroom door and placed my hand on it. I had cried a few times since they had passed, mainly at night when I went to sleep, but I still had a tear or two left for them.

"Thanks for everything," I said quietly before turning and heading out the front door without looking back.

Driving was not as difficult as I had thought it would be, although I'm pretty sure I wouldn't have gotten three feet if it had been a manual. I had managed to reverse the old Honda out of the garage and down the driveway onto the road without hitting anything. Once I was on my way, the stiff steering took a bit to get used to, but the fact that there was no traffic (and probably wouldn't ever be again) helped me get the hang of it. I still didn't have a clear idea of where I wanted to go, so I decided to head on over to Main Street.

Fort Carter is, or rather was, a small town between Providence and Woonsocket. Main Street is the only place that could be considered a business district. There were the customary diners, antique stores, bakeries, and boutiques, along with City Hall, the police and fire stations, a small town museum, and a supermarket. The United General Hospital, where Eleanor had tried to take Alan the day after Christmas, was located out of town, halfway between Fort Carter and Mapleville, the neighboring town.

At the far end of Main Street, where it ended at a T junction with state highway 102, was the newest addition to the town, a Walmart that had opened just six months prior, to much excitement from the locals. I decided to head there but when I spotted the sign for the grocery store in the distance, I thought it might be worth a look. Maybe I could grab some more supplies of the edible kind.

The streets of the town were deserted and dusted in a light snowfall, but I kept my eyes peeled as I drove. At least the red pickup would stand out like a beacon if it was anywhere nearby.

It was surreal. Most of the homes I passed didn't have cars in the driveways and I assumed most people had fled, because the streets were mostly empty of vehicles as well.

When I got to the parking lot of Dave's Marketplace, I saw maybe a half-dozen cars parked there, but from the snow on then, it was obvious they had been there quite a while. There were no lights on anywhere which meant the entire town had lost power, not just our neighborhood.

Pulling up close to the doors of the supermarket, I surveyed the windows looking for signs of movement before finally switching the car off. I got out of the car as quietly as I could and walked to the doors with my hand in my coat pocket on the reassuring shape of the gun. The doors failed to hiss open like they normally did, and for a moment I stood there, perplexed before I remembered the power was out.

How am I going to get them open? I thought.

I placed my hands on either side of the join and attempted to get my fingers between the panes so I could pull them open.

"Isaac ... Isaac Race!"

I jumped as the deep, muffled voice ripped through the frigid silence, and spun around to locate the owner of the voice. Standing at the corner of the building, a tall figure with a strange black face and huge eyes glared at me.

8

I took two hurried steps back, scrabbling to pull the gun from my pocket as the figure stepped forward and reached up to its face, which I only realized then, was covered by a gas mask.

The figure pulled away the mask to reveal the familiar smile and red curls of my classmate, Luke.

"Isaac, it's me, Luke!"

"Luke? Jeez… you scared the hell out of me," I said, regaining my composure. I released the .38's grip, surprised and happy to see someone I actually knew. It was like finding a gold coin in a pile of shit. A small miracle.

Luke seemed to think so too and crossed to me in three big strides, his long arms opened wide. Never one for shows of affection, I stuck my hand out to shake and avoid his embrace, but he was having none of it. He neatly dodged my hand and engulfed me in a bear hug that lifted me clean off my feet.

"Holy crap Isaac, I thought I was the only one left around here," he said, dropping me back to Earth and gripping my shoulders.

"Are you feeling okay?" he asked, looking into my eyes. "No sniffles or aches?"

"Nothing but some cracked ribs thanks to your hug," I said, catching a little of his enthusiasm.

His rich laugh bounced around the empty carpark.

"What are you doing here?" I asked. It was a pretty lame question to ask someone you just found after the end of the world, but it was all I could come up with at short notice.

"Same thing as you, I imagine," he said, grinning. "I came to do some shopping."

"What's with the gas mask? You know you'd already be dead if it was going to kill you, right?"

"Yeah, but I found it in the disposals store and it looked kind of cool ..." He shrugged and threw it aside. I felt kind of mean for calling him out on it. I nodded to the supermarket.

"Is there anything left in there, do you think? It's been over a week since the shit hit the fan." I thought of Alan when I said it, and quickly suppressed the stab of pain it brought with it.

"I hope so, man," he replied. "I ran out of food yesterday and I'm hungry as all get out."

"Well, let's do this then."

Luke had a small hunting knife in a leather case on his belt, and he used it to wedge between the doors and pry them slightly open so that we could get a grip. Working together, we managed to pull them open with some sweating and cussing. Luke reached out and grabbed a shopping cart to wedge between the doors. He knuckle bumped me.

"Ready?"

"Yep," I said, and we scrambled over and entered the dark supermarket.

"It's a good idea to keep our lines of retreat clear," he said, looking back. "Never know what – or who – you might run into."

"The place looks deserted," I replied.

"They always do," he said, with a derisive snort as he led the way down the first aisle. "Dude, haven't you ever played Wasteland Four?"

I grabbed an abandoned cart and we began our 'shopping' in earnest. We stayed away from the produce and meat sections in the last aisles, where the stench of spoiling food was strong, but found the rest of the store surprisingly well-stocked for a week after an apocalypse.

The poorly lit, messy supermarket was a little spooky at first, but Luke made it fun and we were anything but stealthy. We filled my shopping cart with cans of food, and Luke grabbed a second one. He had the presence of mind to fill his cart with as much bottled water as he could. I grabbed a 12-pack of Coke, thinking I might need something to keep me awake when I was travelling.

Of course, being kids, we also hit the candy section ... hard. We cleared entire shelves of M&Ms, Milky Ways, and Snickers (my favorite).

"So, what's your plan once we're stocked up?" Luke asked, as we pushed our carts toward the front doors.

"I'm not sure," I replied. "Do you know if Canada was hit by the attack?"

"Canada's gone man," he said, shaking his head. "Last I heard, everything north of the Southern Mexico border had been hit."

"Damn. So, all that's left of United States is now made up of Hawaii, Guam, and Puerto Rico?"

"I guess so, but I don't think the US still exists at all," he said with a shrug. "I think this is just the North American province of China or something now."

"How could somebody, anybody, do something like this?"

"I don't know, man," he said. "It's pretty messed up."

That was the understatement of all time.

"Hey, if you want, you can hang with me for a while," he said, his face hopeful. "If you want to that is."

"I don't know, I was hoping to get the hell out of town before the Chinese soldiers get here." I didn't mention the looters in the red truck to him. "If they're rounding up kids in the major cities, it's only a matter of time before they start looking in the smaller towns and suburbs."

"Okay, well at least come over until you decide what to do. Besides, it would make it a lot easier to get my stuff there if we use your car."

"Alright then," I replied. "Where's your house?"

"Not my house, man. I've been living at Walt's Diner ever since my parents ..." His voice hitched unexpectedly and he took a second to compose himself. "I've been living there the last few days. Best place in town to hang. It's got a wood-fire grill that they used for cooking their burgers and steaks, so you don't need electricity to cook."

"Smart," I nodded. "Sure, I'll give you a lift, and maybe even stay a night."

"Awesome, man," Luke said. "Now, let's get this stuff loaded."

9

I didn't just stay one night.

Truth is, I didn't want to head out on my own and I'm pretty sure Luke didn't want me to either. We spent the next few days in relative comfort, eating well and watching out for signs of the Chinese army in our area. After four days there had been no dramas, no sign of anyone in fact. It was as if we had the whole town to ourselves.

Luke and I became firm friends. He was a unique character, nerdy but knowledgeable in the ways of the world. While he was obviously a bit of a computer geek, his parents had clearly encouraged him to spend plenty of time outdoors. He knew a lot about everything to do with guns and military. Even history. One time I asked him why he thought the Chinese had done what they had.

"Lebensraum…"

"What?" I looked at him blankly.

"Lebensraum. It's a German word. It means 'living space.' Hitler used it as an excuse for his invasion of other countries in Europe. It was to provide room for the 'superior' races to live as they expanded and took over the world."

"Okay ...?" I frowned, not completely understanding. History had never been my strongest subject.

"Well, think about it," he said, taking on the tone of a teacher. "China has a population of over 1.4 billion people in an area roughly the size of the U.S. That's one billion more than us ... well ... one billion more than we *had*. And everyone knows that the world's population was getting bigger every day. It was going to get pretty grim over the next fifty years. There would have been wars over food, and oil, and probably land."

"Well, why us? Why not somewhere like Australia, which is nearly empty anyway?"

Luke shook his head.

"Isn't it obvious? As much as I hate what they have done, it was a pretty masterful plan. Defeat your only rival superpower, take their land and resources. No one will try and stop you because everyone else is afraid the same thing will happen to them. And it's all here for them once they clear away the dead. Homes, cities, transport. All they gotta do is move in ..."

"Do you think they meant to only kill the adults?"

"That I'm not sure of, but it does make sense if they wanted easy to manage, cost-free labor to help clean up the mess they made."

That particular conversation left me a little depressed. It made a horrible kind of sense. Help was not coming. Would our allies risk their own people for what was left of America? I didn't think so. We were on our own.

We spent much of those few days in the diner's kitchen where the wood burning grill provided not only a place to cook, but also heat to stave off the cold Rhode Island winter. Although the temperature had climbed above freezing, allowing what remained of the snow to melt away, it had not cracked 40 degrees and was dropping well below freezing at night.

Luckily for us, old Walt had kept a good supply of firewood on hand. It was stacked beneath a tarp against the wall in the alley behind the diner. Not wanting to advertise our presence, I'd parked the car in that same alley, so on those few occasions that we did leave the diner, we always came and went by the back door.

Although we did talk about moving on, the warmth and safety of the diner meant we became a little complacent and the urgency to move on gradually faded.

On the morning of our fifth day together at the diner, I was out in the main dining room raiding the peppermint candies that sat next to the register while Luke slept in back. I was about to put one in my mouth when I glimpsed a flash of red from the corner of my eye.

Turning my head I saw a familiar red pickup truck cruising down Main Street past the diner. I ducked fast and crept to the window, watching as it pulled to a stop in front of the hardware store three doors down.

There were a bunch of scared looking kids in the back. I counted six, both boys and girls and none looked older than twelve. They sat quietly as the driver, the older teen from before, and his younger partner in crime got out. The looters both carried the same shotguns I had seen them with in the Fosters' street.

There was no sign of the man I'd shot in the leg. Probably the sickness (or the bullet wound) had claimed him. The driver went to the back of the truck and lowered the tailgate. The kids cringed away from him.

"Hey, man, what's up?" Luke called from behind me. I quickly turned and waved him to silence and beckoned him to the window. He was by my side in a flash and crouched down beside me.

"Those guys came through looting our neighborhood before I left my foster parents' house," I spoke quietly.

"No kidding, what happened?"

"I shot one of them and they took off," I said, without taking my eyes off the pickup.

"You did what!?"

If I hadn't been concentrating on the scene outside I might have smiled at his absolute surprise.

"I shot one. Well, it was kind of an accid…"

"You have a gun?"

"Yeah, it's in the pocket on the front of my coat," I said, glancing at him sheepishly. "Sorry, I was going to tell you but I forgot."

He didn't seem too fussed.

"Should we go get it?" he asked.

We watched as the older teen herded three of the kids from the back of the truck toward the hardware store. The kids went on ahead while he followed them with his shotgun at the ready. Obviously they were now using the kids to collect supplies faster.

The younger teen stayed with the three kids still in the back of the Toyota, resting against the dray with his shotgun between his legs as he lit a cigarette.

"I guess we better have it, just in case they try to get in here," I replied. "You keep an eye out and I'll go get it."

He nodded and I crossed the dining room at a crouch, heading into the kitchen.

My stuff was piled in the corner by the door to the alley and I realized how foolish I had been to leave the revolver there. What if the looters had come here first? What if they had come through the back door while we were out front? It was a frightening idea. I didn't want to end up as a slave to anybody, not the Chinese, and certainly not to a couple of goons with shotguns.

I had just pulled the revolver from the pocket of my coat when I heard a gunshot from out front. Even in a building and a hundred feet away, it was shockingly loud.

.38 in hand, I rushed back to the door into the dining area where I saw Luke flattened to the floor beneath the window. He waved for me to keep back and I stepped back into the darkened kitchen just as the younger of the shotgun-wielding looters sprinted by the diner's front window.

I heard another shot. This one much louder and from the alley beside the restaurant. Luke crawled across the dining room floor to join me just inside the kitchen.

"The three kids that the younger guy was watching made a break for it as soon as the others were in the hardware store," Luke said, breathlessly. "They ran this way."

"Come on," I replied, pulling him back into the kitchen. "Grab a knife or something and we'll watch the back door of this place in case he looks for them in here."

Luke grabbed a wicked foot-long chef's knife from the block at the food preparation counter and hurried over to the door where my stuff lay scattered. From there, he'd be hidden behind the door as it opened. I moved to squat behind the end of the grill where I had a clear view of both the back door and the door to the dining room. The revolver again seemed unnaturally heavy in my sweaty hand.

A full minute passed, then another. I was just starting to think that the danger had passed when the back door handle began to turn. Taking a deep breath, I pointed the revolver at the door and tried to decide if I should just shoot through it or not.

Luke raised a hand to stop me and quietly placed the knife on the linoleum floor. He stepped to the door and yanked it open to reveal a pale-faced girl, her blue eyes wide in surprise. Luke clapped a hand over her mouth and pulled her into the kitchen, grappling with her frantic wriggling as he shut and locked the door with his free hand.

I didn't recognize her. She was a few years younger than us, probably 10 or 11. She was whimpering and struggling to escape Luke's grip.

I put my gun on the counter and went across to them.

"It's okay," I said, my hands spread in what I hoped was a non-threatening manner. "We aren't going to hurt you. But you have to be quiet or the boy that was chasing you might hear. Okay?"

She still looked frightened, but nodded.

"I'm going to take my hand away now," said Luke calmly. "Don't scream or he'll find us."

Luke took his hand away.

"Who are ..." she started to say, but was cut off by Luke's hand again. He put a finger over his lips and shook his head before taking his hand away again.

"I think he's in the alley," Luke whispered as he leaned in close over us. We strained to hear what might be happening.

I heard it first, or at least I reacted to it first, looking up toward the ceiling and then back down at Luke. It was a distant rumble that was growing louder by the second. Soon the chop, chop, chop blades cutting through the air was unmistakable. A helicopter. Big by the sounds of it. The rumble closed overhead and grew until it made utensils and plates in the kitchen tremble.

There was a frightened shout from the alleyway.

"Sounds like he's running," I said.

Luke nodded, his eyes bright with excitement or fear. He looked at the girl.

"I'm Luke and this is Isaac," he said quickly, answering the question he had silenced with his hand. "We need to move."

"Come on, and stay down," I said, and headed toward the dining room.

The younger of the two armed looters was crouched twenty feet away under a bus shelter. If he had heard us while he was in the alleyway, he didn't show it, focused as he was on getting back to his pickup truck.

We cautiously made our way to the window and watched as he darted from under the cover of the shelter and sprinted for the truck. The driver was already herding the kids he had taken into the hardware store into the back of the truck.

"Hurry the hell up!" he yelled to his partner as he slammed the tailgate closed and ran to the driver's door.

The kid barely managed to jump into the back of the truck before his partner started the truck and tore off down the street. The children in the back were huddling in fear while the armed kid leaned defiantly on the back of the cab and raised his middle finger in salute.

We couldn't see the helicopter from our position, it was too high above the street, but the roar of the engine told us it was following them. Then the kid made a mistake. His last.

He raised his shotgun skyward.

"Don't do it idiot!" rasped Luke.

He did. The shotgun kicked in his hand.

Somewhere overhead I heard a whining roar and willed the pickup to go faster.

Do you know how, in the movies, a line of machine gun fire will leave little pockmarks in the road as it creeps toward a target? That didn't happen. Instead a section of road about two and half feet wide was pulverized to powder by the rapid fire ammunition that began to make a deadly beeline at the fleeing vehicle. It reached them in barely a second.

"No!" I screamed, thinking of the helpless kids as the truck was sawed in half by the withering fire. I lost sight of them in the flying debris and dust. That is something I am eternally thankful for.

My heartbeat thudded in my ears as we waited under the window. Would the chopper land and its occupants search the area? If so, we were toast. From the look that Luke gave me, I could tell he was thinking the same thing. Finally, after circling for what seemed like an hour but was, in fact, probably only five minutes, the chopper flew off. It was then I noticed the gentle sobbing between Luke and me.

I looked down at the girl, but left it to Luke to comfort her. I was too angry at the massacre I had just witnessed to do anything else.

I knew that the time had come to leave but after seeing the fate of the truck, I was not sure that driving was the best idea. I still had no idea where to go and neither did Luke, although somewhere during that few days we came to an unspoken agreement we would go together.

Surprisingly it was the girl who helped us come up with a destination.

10

Her name was Sarah and that afternoon, as we got over the shock of what we'd witnessed, she revealed that she and her friends had come from Providence. Barbara, an older girl, had been driving them north to some sort of refuge when the looters in the red truck had ambushed them a couple of miles outside of Fort Carter.

Sarah was obviously traumatized by her recent experiences, so getting information out of her was like pulling teeth, but, over the course of the next few hours, we managed to learn the important parts of her story. Sarah and her friends had been at a Bible School Christmas retreat which was supposed to last from the day after Christmas until New Year's Eve.

The last time she had ever seen her parents was when they put her on the bus to be taken to the retreat. Speaking of them brought a fresh bout of tears, but she persevered with her story after some coaxing. The four adult camp counselors, some already coughing when they arrived, had all been sick by the time night fell and had left in a car to seek medical attention after serving dinner. They left the younger children in the care of Barbara, a 16-year old high school student who was counseling at the camp for the first time.

They didn't come back. Phones didn't work. A snowstorm hit.

"Barbara was so nice. Really smart too and she looked after us, but we were all freaking out. She kept telling us help would come but it never did."

When New Year's Day arrived with no contact from the outside world, the children had confronted Barbara. They knew she had been hiding the worst of what had happened from them, knew she had been watching the TV for updates when she could.

She didn't deny it. She had kept silent while their whole world was swept away by the biological strike but when the airwaves went dead and it was clear that no one was coming, she told the children everything.

She had comforted them, letting them know God was still watching over them. I felt a bitter stab at that, but didn't say anything, not wanting to upset Sarah any more than she was already.

It was Barbara who had found the message while cycling through the static of silent radio waves. She was looking for news or music or anything to prove that they weren't alone.

On one particular frequency, the static would be interrupted by a series of beeps every hour and the beeping would last no more than three minutes at a time. A ten-year-old boy called Johnny said it sounded like Morse code. He said he had studied it in Scouts and tried writing out the message. It didn't seem to make any sense. At least, not until Barbara realized that it was written backwards.

Sarah couldn't remember the exact message, but she remembered enough for us to get excited. She remembered it was about a place, a safe haven in New Hampshire.

"It said something about going to the dragon too, but we couldn't work out what that meant. Barbara was sure it was from the government or something," Sarah said.

I saw doubt scrawled on Luke's face but he kept his thoughts to himself.

We asked more questions. Barbara had been adamant that the safe haven was the answer to their prayers. Literally. To her, this Morse code message had seemed like a sign from God and she told the children as much. Sarah believed it fervently.

"We have to go there. All the children of America will be gathering there to stay safe and start over."

I had never met Barbara, but I had to give it to her, she knew how to sell an idea. Turns out she had no clue where it actually was, but the plan had been to head to New Hampshire and worry about the rest later.

The day after the Morse code had been decoded Barbara had loaded the kids into the church bus and started the trek north to New Hampshire. They were just entering Fort Carter when the red Toyota had run them off the road and the looters had taken them prisoner. From Sarah's memory that had been January 4th, the same day that I had ventured into town to find supplies and met Luke.

The looters had taken their captives to a trailer park where they had apparently made their base. Sarah wouldn't tell us about what had happened while she was a prisoner, other than to say that the oldest looter had taken Barbara off to a separate trailer almost as soon as they had arrived. The kids had never seen her again.

Every day since, the looters had put them in the pickup and taken them on scavenger runs. I didn't want to think about what had happened to Barbara. Was she still captive in one of the trailers? Or worse, dead? Sarah had no idea where the trailer park was but I didn't think it would be too hard to find.

We listened to the last of her story.

They had been on a scavenger run that morning and the stop near Walt's Diner had been the first of the day. While the younger looter had been busy smoking, his shotgun resting against his leg, Johnny, the same kid who had deciphered the Morse Code, had nodded to her and the seven-year old boy, Brent, to make a run for it. Johnny had been talking about escaping for days, but this was the first opportunity they'd had where they weren't either bound or being watched over properly.

The shotgun-toting delinquent, clearly not as distracted as they thought, had shot Brent in the back as they ran towards the diner. Sarah and Johnny managed to make it into the alleyway but Johnny had stumbled and fallen. His last words to Sarah had been to tell her to keep running.

His death was the result of the second shot I had heard while retrieving the revolver.

"I made it out the back and hid behind a dumpster," Sarah said. "Then when he stopped and started going through the stuff in the car out back, I snuck back and tried the door. That's when you found me."

There was an old radio in the kitchen. Luke and I had never turned it on, but after hearing Sarah's story, he checked it and found the batteries still worked. We moved the station bar around for a while, looking for anything other than static, but found ourselves getting no place fast.

"Maybe the place ... this dragon safe place, has been taken out by the Chinese already?" Luke said.

"Just a little bit longer," I said, moving on to another station frequency. "It was a church retreat, right? Maybe they were listening to AM."

"Nobody listens to AM radio, man," Luke said, looking at me incredulously.

"My foster mother did, on Thursday evenings, AM-1107 used to have a gospel hour."

"Alright, we can try it if you want."

I pushed the button that switched the radio from FM to AM and began slowly cycling through the frequencies. Nothing. I cycled through the dials twice and was ready to give up.

"Remember it didn't play all the time. It came on about every five minutes," she said. "Don't give up yet."

I dialed through again three times, ignoring Luke's sighs. On the third time, the radio beeped as I cycled through.

"Go back!" yelled Luke and Sarah in perfect unison.

We had found it. The broadcast was just as Sarah had described – a sequence of long and short beeps. I knew nothing about Morse code and although Luke had been a Scout he didn't have a clue either. There was no way we could decipher it, so we simply accepted that the message would be largely the same as Sarah had relayed it to us. For now, that was good enough.

Luke and I sat down at a table in the dining room while an exhausted Sarah slept fitfully in the kitchen.

"We have to go there, right?"

"Sure, maybe … I'm not sure. You do realize New Hampshire is two states away? And we don't have even a rough idea of where in the state it might be."

"Do we have a choice? Do you want to wait here for the Chinese ground troops as we run out of food?"

"No – it's just – it might really suck is all."

"Oh, it's going to suck alright," I replied. "Especially as we'll have to walk it."

"What! Why?"

"I think the Chinese are looking for moving vehicles, probably with satellites or something. I don't think it's a coincidence that the first moving vehicle we've seen in days shows up a few minutes before a Chinese chopper. I don't know about you, but I don't really want to be driving if it's a possibility we'll end up like…" I waved vaguely in the direction of the street.

Luke grimaced.

"It could have been a coincidence," he said quietly.

"Do you want to risk it?" I asked.

"Fine, we walk. We're gonna need some warmer clothes though," he said, picking at his t-shirt.

"Yep, our first stop's gonna be Walmart. Hopefully it's as well stocked as the grocery store was. Now, what about this 'dragon' in the message? Maybe we can work it out and find it on a map."

"Okay, I'll think on it," he said. "We should be able to pick up a map or an atlas at Walmart."

Luke packed up food to take with us on the road while I carried a linen tablecloth from the diner's storeroom and went out to the alley. Sarah's friend Johnny was face down on the cold, hard concrete near the entrance.

It was the third dead body I'd seen in a week and it didn't get any easier. In fact, this was worse. Much worse. As upsetting as it was seeing the lifeless bodies of people I loved, this was just a poor little kid. The waste of innocent life hit me hard.

Tears stung my eyes as I knelt and draped the tablecloth over him. I sat back on my haunches and took a deep breath, cursing the Chinese and the dumb cruelty of the looters.

I put my hand gently on the shape of his head. I was in no mood to say a prayer.

"Rest in peace, buddy," I said hoarsely, before heading back inside.

Part Two

WE HIT THE ROAD

11

Although we dressed as warmly as we could, we didn't end up taking a lot of food with us when we left Walt's Diner. We had decided that travelling light was preferable to lugging overladen bags. Besides, Sarah was suddenly reluctant to leave the warmth and safety of the diner even though it was her who initially encouraged us to head for New Hampshire. Carrying a heavy pack would only make the journey worse for her.

I remember the hard, practical side of me thinking it might be better to leave her behind, to just slip away while she slept ... but I could never suggest that course of action. It wasn't right, and I knew it only crossed my mind because I was annoyed at the delay.

Luke played the Barbara card and managed to convince Sarah that it was for the best.

"Its what Barb would want."

"We will we go look for her, right?" Sarah asked, as we got set to leave.

"Sure," Luke said, before meeting my eye. "I'm pretty sure I know which trailer park it is."

We hadn't discussed it, but I knew it was the right thing to do. Besides, I wanted to make up for the horrible thought I'd had about leaving Sarah behind.

The walk to Walmart took us past the shredded remains of the red pickup. We steered Sarah to the far side of the street and Luke and I walked between her and the wreckage to obstruct her view. It was hard not to look at the remains of the truck, which had been literally shredded by the high caliber rounds.

"I think I see something, keep going," Luke said, before darting across the road to the wreck.

"Watch it, there's a ton of glass and sharp metal," I called, wondering what he had spied as I gently propelled Sarah onward.

"Yep," he said.

I watched over my shoulder as he ran to the other sidewalk and the far reaches of the debris and bent over. To my surprise he stood and held up one of the looter's shotguns triumphantly. Miraculously, it appeared undamaged.

"It's a pump action 20-gauge," he said, as he caught up with us and handed it to me. "Must have been thrown clear, it barely has a scratch on it. My dad and I used a gun just like this for duck hunting last year. I'm not going to dig through that mess for extra ammo though; hopefully we can find some at Walmart."

"I wouldn't mind an extra box of bullets for my .38, too," I said, handing it back before looking up and down the street. "Come on, let's get going."

"Am I going to get a gun, too?" Sarah asked, looking frightened by the prospect.

"No, guns are dangerous," I replied, thinking back to the first time I had fired one, hitting the sick looter in the leg. "Luke and I will be able to protect you just fine. You don't need a weapon."

We continued down Main Street toward Walmart. It was a walk of about four blocks from the wrecked pickup. The wind picked up, its cutting chill piercing right through my coat and the sweatshirt I wore underneath. I hoped that I could find a more heavy-duty jacket at Walmart, perhaps one designed for ski trips or Arctic conditions.

By the time we reached the end of Main, I was starting to second-guess my decision to not take the car. Would it be worse dying in a shriek of twisting metal and hot raining lead or freezing to death in a ditch on the way to New Hampshire?

One look at Highway 102 validated the decision. While in town, the streets had been relatively clear of vehicles, but the highway was absolutely littered with them. It looked like anybody that could drive had tried to escape town and been caught up in the largest traffic jam in history. There was no way we would find a clear path for a vehicle of our own.

"Damn ..." Luke said, shaking his head. I waited for him to continue his thought, but he lapsed into silence. I wondered if, like me, he was pondering how many had succumbed to the illness and died in their cars as they tried to escape.

"I guess there's no need to look both ways before crossing," I said, starting across the highway toward Walmart's parking lot. I meant to be funny, but it just came out weak.

"What if there are more bad people like Bradley, the guy who had us in the truck?" Sarah asked, grabbing my arm from behind. "They could be waiting for us in Walmart ... it's a perfect place to trap people."

"There could be bad people any place," I said, trying to sound reassuring. I could tell that the poor girl was on the edge of breaking into tears again. "We need to get supplies from this place or we can't head to the safe haven. It's a risk we're going to have to take."

"Besides, if anybody tries to hurt you, they've got another thing comin'," Luke said, holding up his shotgun. I felt a ping of dismay as I recalled how useless the kid's shotgun had proven to be against the helicopter.

The glass of the large front door had been smashed in. We stopped at the threshold and I kept my hand on the gun in my pocket as we surveyed the scene. We could tell at once that some looting had been done here. Items were scattered all over the floor and in places, the shelves had been pushed over. Still, it seemed to be well-stocked.

I was creeped out that day and, even now, I still haven't gotten used to empty stores; they are like haunted houses, places that once bustled with people on errands and day-to-day tasks. Remnants of the world that was.

I stepped through the smashed opening, careful not to cut myself on the glass around the edges and waved the others through. Once inside, we stopped to listen for anything that might indicate we weren't alone in the dark store.

"I think it's safe. Want to split up, or stick together?" I whispered. That's the other thing, even though you know these places are empty, you always feel the impulse to stay quiet.

"Together for now," Luke said, looking as spooked as I felt. "It might take us a bit longer, but I don't think Sarah should be out of sight. We're not in a hurry and I don't know about you, but I'm happy to be out of the wind for a while."

"Yep. Okay, where should we start?"

"Girls' clothing," he said, nodding toward Sarah. "She's by far the most under-dressed of us for this weather."

"Girls' clothing it is," I said. "After that, some warmer clothes for us and a trip to the camping section might be in order."

It didn't take us long to get Sarah bundled up with some good winter clothing, including a pair of galoshes, some extra pants and thermal shirts. We put them in a new backpack for her. She was mostly quiet, nodding her head or shaking it as we suggested various items of clothing to her.

Looking back, it's easy to see that she was still in shock from what she had seen, heck, from everything that had happened to her. In reality we were probably all in shock, but I guess my history was helping me to adapt more readily than would otherwise be the case. As for Luke, well, apart from the slight crack in his voice when he mentioned his parents, he seemed to have weathered the storm remarkably well. I figured he was just made of sterner stuff than most.

I know better now. Luke wasn't unaffected, it's just that he did a good job of hiding it, and the things I've seen him do since convince me has the heart of a hero. It sounds corny, but I'm grateful we found each other after the Flu. I'm not sure that either of us would still be here if we hadn't.

I grabbed a couple extra pairs of wool socks and a quilted parka for myself. Other than that, I didn't take too long gathering extra clothing, as I already had some good warm clothing in my pack.

Luke grabbed a few pairs of 'Long Johns,' as he liked to call thermal underwear, and at his insistence I pakked a pair for myself as well.

"You never know," he said. "These Long Johns could save your life someday."

After gathering our clothing, we headed to the back of the store to look at camping gear. This part of the store had been more thoroughly picked over, but I still hoped to find a tent that was light enough for one of us to carry. I didn't relish the idea of sleeping exposed to the elements in the New England winter if we couldn't find a house.

While I looked for a tent, Luke went over to sporting goods, the next section over, to look for ammunition. I sent Sarah into the next aisle to look for sleeping bags.

Her scream caught me completely off guard.

12

Tearing around the corner with my revolver in my hand, I almost collided with Sarah as she backed up, still shrieking. A boy and girl about my age were standing at the far end of the aisle, each holding a bow with an arrow nocked to the string.

Both were aiming at me.

I shoved Sarah behind me and stepped forward, trying to appear much braver than I felt, with the .38 raised.

"I was just trying to ask her name," the boy said in a clipped accent, as he eyed my handgun warily.

"Perhaps we should ask yours?" Luke's question from behind them was punctuated by the sound of the shotgun's pump racking. "Drop the bows and we'll have a friendly chat."

A look of frustration crossed the boy's face. He was clearly upset at having been outmaneuvered, but his arrow stayed unwaveringly trained on me. It was the girl, who shared the same proud features and blonde hair as him, who lowered her weapon.

He glanced at her and she nodded.

"We don't have a choice."

The boy slowly lowered his bow.

"Good move," said Luke. "Now un-knock the arrows and put your bows on the floor."

They followed the order, the boy looking more and more uncomfortable at the turn of events. I couldn't blame him, if the situation had been reversed and I had the guns of strangers trained on me I would have been terrified.

The boy eyed us defiantly as Luke skirted them and joined Sarah and I. The girl simply smiled and said, "Well, this is awkward isn't it?"

That's how we met Ben and Brooke.

Ben and Brooke are twins, both tall, good looking and blonde. Although they aren't identical (I guess that's obvious, how could they be when one's a guy and the other's a girl?), they do look alike. They also tend to think alike. Not only that, they are English, having come to the United States to spend Christmas with their maternal grandparents. They sure picked the wrong year to take that holiday.

Tension was thick there in the Walmart at that first meeting and things could have ended up very differently had the twins, especially Brooke, not been so level-headed.

"You chaps look a little tense, can we offer you something to eat?" said Brooke.

"Sure, why not," said Luke, immediately and lowered his gun, smiling goofily at the pretty English girl.

I looked at him incredulously.

"What?" He said defensively. "They're obviously decent people."

I shook my head with a grin and pocketed my own weapon.

The twins, Ben still looking a little leery of us, took us back to their 'lair', the employee break room. They did their best to make us feel welcome and we shared a cold meal and spoke of our experiences.

Their grandparents had succumbed to the Flu quikkly and the twins had stayed in their home as long as they could before hunger had forced them to leave.

While they were realists, they were still hopeful that the rest of the world wouldn't just let the 'bloody' Chinese get away with it and that, at some point, they would be reunited with their parents.

As soon as we mentioned travelling to the safe haven we had heard about, they wanted in. Ben even had a solution to the walking problem: bicycles. Walmart had a huge range of bicycles.

"Do we have any idea where this place is located?" asked Ben after we finished picking out bikes.

"Not really, have you remembered anything else about the message, Sarah?" I asked, turning to her.

"Not really," she replied. "Barbara just kept talking about the 'dragon' clue. She said we would look for it when we got to New Hampshire. That's all I can remember ... wait! There was something about the dragon being on a white mountain!"

"Dragon on a white mountain? Sounds like something from *The Hobbit*," said Brooke.

"There's a White Mountain National Forest in New Hampshire!" Luke said and grabbed the atlas he had found in the book section of the store. We all stood up and hovered over the table as he leafed through the pages until he found New Hampshire. "See? It's huge though. It almost cuts the state in half. Unless we have more details, it'll be like trying to find a needle in a haystack."

"Well done, Luke, that's a start," I said. "Unless someone has a better idea of where to go or what to do, I vote that we should head there. Maybe there'll be other travelers. Surely we can't be the only ones that heard the message."

"Neither of you happen to be good with Morse code, do you?" Luke asked, glancing back at the twins. They shook their heads.

"Alright then," I said. "Let's find some baskets for these bikes. That way we can carry more supplies. I think we should leave in the morning and head north. Agreed?"

No one dissented.

"We should avoid big cities if we want to avoid the Chinese army," said Brooke, and we all agreed.

"It looks like we can avoid Woonsocket," Luke said, after turning the atlas back to a map of Rhode Island. Woonsocket was the nearest 'city'. It was much bigger than Fort Carter but would barely rate as a city in some of the other states. He flipped to the Massachusetts page. "It doesn't look like we'll be able to skirt around Worcester as easily though."

With a little over two hundred thousand people, Worcester was a real city, the second largest in New England after Boston.

"If we have to go through, we will," I said. "But maybe something else will come up before we get there."

"Sounds like a plan, man," Luke said, closing the atlas. "I think I'll hold onto this. It could come in handy."

"We should grab another one, too," Brooke said. "A backup never hurts."

"Great idea!" said Luke, a little too enthusiastically.

Boy he had it bad.

13

The sun rose the next morning to find us preparing to leave Walmart. We were all packed. Each of us had a full backpack and bike baskets loaded with supplies. I loaded the shotgun ammo I found into my backpack as Luke wasn't around.

"Where is Luke?" Ben asked.

"I think he went to the bathroom," Sarah replied. "Here he is."

Luke emerged from one of the aisles holding up a box proudly.

"Crossbow," he said, and knelt on the floor.

He began to rip open the cardboard packaging. At first, I thought it was a toy, but when he pulled out the camouflage-patterned weapon I saw that it was indeed real, as were the short arrows, or bolts, or whatever they called them. He slung the crossbow over his shoulder and secured the Velcro belt of eight holstered arrows to his thigh.

"Where did you find that?" Ben asked. "I could do with one of those, too. The bows are too big and clumsy to take with us."

"Sorry, this was the last one. It was tucked behind a counter. All the shelves were cleaned out, probably in the panic after the outbreak. Here, you can have this though."

He handed Ben the shotgun. The English boy took it gingerly.

"Don't worry, the safety is on," Luke said.

I wasn't sure about giving up a firearm for what was essentially a medieval weapon, but I could tell from the loving way he handled it that Luke wouldn't be persuaded to give the crossbow up. We got started not long after.

A mile down Highway 102, it crossed the Quaker Highway which would lead us, after another half-mile or so, to the Providence-Worcester Turnpike. This would give us a fairly straight shot across the semi-rugged and forested southern Massachusetts countryside.

It was cold and overcast as we left Walmart's parking lot, weaving our bikes between the silent cars that littered the highway. It started to snow even before we reached the turnpike.

"This could be some tough sleddin', Boss," Luke said, pedaling up beside me. "Bicycles can be hard to ride in the snow."

"Nothing we can do about it now," I replied. "If it gets too bad, we'll find someplace to stop until it lets up."

"What if it doesn't let up 'til spring?" he asked. "It's still January, after all."

"Heck, I don't know ... maybe we'll come across a place with snowmobiles."

The snow did let up before it started sticking to the road, but that conversation with Luke kept playing on my mind. Somehow, I was beginning to feel responsible, not only for myself, but for our entire ragtag little group. What if I led them astray? The thought nagged at me as we rode.

It was 19 miles from where we got on the turnpike to the edge of Worcester, and we planned on staying on it the entire way.

We had only been on the turnpike for three or so miles when Brooke's keen eyesight caught something coming toward us. We had just passed an off ramp, so we turned our bikes around and hightailed it back before speeding down the ramp and hiding in the bushes near the underpass.

We watched the turnpike from our hideout, the others looking as apprehensive as I felt. Five minutes later, a bulldozer and two trucks came into view. They were moving slowly, the dozer making sure the breakdown lane was clear, pushing the occasional abandoned vehicle out of the way. Behind them rumbled four tanks. American tanks! I could see the flags, and with a surge of joy I started up from our hiding position, ready to wave them down. Luke grabbed me by the sleeve and pulled me roughly to the ground.

"Dude," he whispered harshly. "Look at the sentry!"

One of the tanks had its hatch open and the soldier leaning out of it was clearly Asian. That didn't mean a whole lot, but the flag on the shoulder of his bluish camouflage uniform was an unmistakable blotch of red.

A glance into the truck cabins confirmed it. Chinese soldiers. I nodded sheepishly, aware of just how close I had come to getting us all captured, or worse, killed.

"I bet they're taking any American military hardware they find," Luke said.

We watched as the tanks continued past, followed by a few more trucks, and finally a single Jeep. A man with a pair of binoculars stood up in the back of the Jeep looking around at the edges of the road. My breath caught as his gaze swept over us and, in my mind at least, seemed to linger just a bit too long.

I held my breath. Finally, the man turned his attention to the other side of the turnpike as the Jeep rolled on. I exhaled sharply. I wasn't the only one.

"Holy crap, that was close," Luke said.

"I wonder if there'll be more of them using that motorway," Ben wondered aloud.

"Luke, does your map show a way to get to Worcester from here without taking the turnpike?" I asked, keeping my eyes on the road.

We waited while he rummaged around for the atlas in his pack.

"Yeah," he said, after opening it to the page he wanted. "But it's going to be longer and take us through a lot of farmland and some small towns."

"Longer I can deal with, if it helps us avoid patrols," said Brooke.

"I'm hungry. Can we stop and eat something?" Sarah asked.

Typical kid, I thought, ignoring the fact that my own stomach was rumbling.

"Let's get a bit further down this road away from the turnpike and we'll stop," I said.

"Looks like we follow this road about half a mile and then turn left," Luke said. "That looks like a good spot to stop for a rest and some grub."

"Okay, let's go," I said.

It was just after noon and we were leaving the small town of North Uxbridge when we noticed we were being followed by dogs. It was, of course, Brooke who spotted them first.

"We have company," she said, pulling up.

They followed at a distance, a pack of mangy dogs of different breeds, but all of them had a lean and hungry look. I could make out at least one Alsatian and there were two other big dogs whose breeds I couldn't identify. They didn't come close to us that afternoon, just followed behind, sniffing at our trail.

"They look terrible," Sarah said when we stopped to rest a couple hours after we first noticed them. "Who's been taking care of them, you know, since the Flu killed all the grown-ups?"

"Probably no one," Luke responded. "That's probably why they are so skinny."

"Maybe we should feed them," Sarah said, sadness creeping into her voice.

"We've barely got enough for ourselves, love," Brooke said, putting a comforting hand on Sarah's shoulder.

"Besides, if you feed a stray, it'll follow you around forever," Luke said. "At least that's what my dad always said."

"I hope they bugger off. I think they are creepy," Ben said, mirroring my own feelings.

Feeding them was the last thing I wanted to do. The thought of them being close enough to handfeed terrified me in an irrational way. I had been bitten by my grandmother's Collie when I was six and still had the scar from a puncture wound on my wrist.

"We aren't going near them," I said, "And tonight we are going to find a place with doors we can lock to sleep in."

When we stopped for the night a couple of hours later, it was just starting to get dark. We found a farmhouse with a large detached garage behind it. The house was locked up tight, and I don't think any of us fancied breaking in. Besides, the garage door was wide open, so we wheeled our bicycles inside and pulled the big roller door down behind us.

A couple windows above a workbench on one wall allowed the dying sunlight to filter in as we set out up our bedding. We ate a meal of beef jerky and potato chips as the sun went down, and by the time we finished it was pitch black in the garage.

Both Ben and Brooke had thought to bring flashlights, but to save on our limited supply of batteries we had decided not to use them unless there was an emergency.

The dogs began howling and barking sometime in the middle of the night. We could hear them growling and scratching at the garage door before what sounded like a vicious fight broke out and ended in high pitched yelping.

No one slept much after that. A whimpering Sarah curled up next to Brooke, the English girl doing her best to comfort her, while Luke and I sat upright with our weapons close by. Ben was ready with his flashlight should the sound of breaking glass or splintering wood be heard.

The sound of the dogs finally died down just as dawn was breaking. I heard one final sniff under the roller door before they disappeared. Everybody but Luke and I fell into a fitful sleep.

"We should let them sleep a while," Luke said. "We can get started again in a few hours."

"Okay, everybody's exhausted from yesterday's ride and last night's ... excitement," I replied, stifling a yawn.

"You should sleep, too," he said. "I can keep watch."

"Are you sure?"

"No sweat, man. I picked up a few energy drinks before we left Walmart. If I feel myself crashing I'll just slam one of them."

"Alright, if you're sure ..."

I got into my sleeping bag and shuffled till I was comfortable. Well, as comfortable as one could be lying on a concrete floor. My eyes closed for what seemed like just a second and suddenly I was being shaken awake. I glanced around in bewilderment.

Everybody else was up and had their sleeping bags repacked.

"What ...?"

"It's about noon," Luke said. "Time to rise and shine, sleepyhead."

"Okay, okay," I muttered, shaking my head, trying to clear the cobwebs from my mind. Sometimes I think a little sleep is worse than none. I got up and stretched. I wasn't quite as exhausted as I had been, but still felt like I'd been worked over by a burly man with a baseball bat. Muscles that I never knew I had were aching. I rolled up my sleeping bag and tied it before returning it to the basket on the front of my bike.

"Any sign of the dogs?" I asked.

"Nope," Luke replied. "When Ben woke up, I got him to watch my back while I went outside to take a wizz and have a look around. They must have found something better to do."

"Well, then we should probably be heading out. We've already wasted too much daylight as it is."

"I figure we've got maybe five hours of light left," Luke said. "We might be able to make it to Worcester by nightfall."

Luke was getting ready to pull up the door when we heard the first thrum of a helicopter in the distance. I motioned for him to leave it closed and he nodded. The chopper flew low over the house and garage we were in and, in truth, I was waiting for huge bullets to begin tearing the garage apart at any moment, but after what seemed like an eternity it moved off into the distance.

"Are they going to come back?" Sarah asked.

"I don't know, but maybe we should wait a while before leaving. I don't want them to catch us riding down the road if they fly back this way."

"If we wait too long, we won't make it very far before dark, man," Luke said.

"Maybe we shouldn't try," I responded, conscious of my aching muscles. "We could wait out the day here, spend another night and leave early in the morning."

"As you Yanks would say, I'm down with that," Ben said, massaging the back of his leg.

"Please, can we?" Sarah asked, her eyes brightening slightly for the first time since I had met her.

"Wouldn't bother me," Brooke chimed in.

"You're the boss," Luke said, shrugging. He pulled the sleeping bag off of his bicycle basket. "If we're staying here though, I'm going to get some shut eye. I'm bushed."

"I'm not the boss," I said.

"It's just a figure of speech, man," Luke said, shrugging before unrolling his sleeping bag onto the floor. "I'll take the watch tonight."

"You do kind of take charge and act bossy," said Sarah, smiling, with a nod of her head.

The way she said it made it sound like it wasn't a bad thing.

14

It was cold in the garage and we spent most of the day cocooned in our sleeping bags and talking quietly. We were out of the wind, which was a blessing, but a fire was out of the question. Luke slept most of the afternoon, and toward late afternoon I also nodded off.

I awoke just before nightfall, when the dogs returned. We could hear them growling and snarling as they scratched at the garage door. That night we were more secure in the safety of our shelter and the rest of my group, including Luke, even managed to get to sleep despite the dogs yammering at the door.

I couldn't, however, and was awake until well after midnight with the .38 in my hand, listening to the pack. Luke awoke in those early hours and took my gun, telling me to sleep. I didn't protest. I was pretty exhausted by then.

Once again, the dogs were gone before first light. We had a quick breakfast of cold beans and were ready to go within a half-hour of the sun cresting the horizon. We hit the road, riding carefully to avoid patches of black ice. Sometime before midday it began snowing again, this time harder. When we stopped to have lunch in a clear spot under some trees, I worried that we wouldn't be able to make it too much further on our bikes.

"Where are we?" I asked Luke, who'd spent most of our lunch stop studying the map of Massachusetts in his atlas.

"Based on that last big crossroad, I'm guessing that we're someplace right about here," he said, jabbing at a spot on the map with his finger. "We're probably five or six miles from Worcester; should make it there in another hour and a half, maybe a bit longer if the weather keeps being a dick."

"Now might be a good time to discuss what we do when we get there," Brooke said. "Worcester's a city and there are bound to be Chinese military there. It's probably where that chopper was headed yesterday."

"I know, I'd prefer to go around it but that might not be possible given the weather," I said.

"Going around would take us too far out of the way," Luke chimed in. "A stealth run through it has to be the best way. It would save us time and distance."

"Both paths are risky," Ben said. "But, given the weather especially, I would think we should try to get through Worcester as soon as possible. If that means dodging Chinese patrols then so be it, but we should wait and make a go of it after dark."

Luke nodded.

"It would be easier to avoid the patrols that way."

"Let's get to the outskirts of town and make our decision then," I replied.

Going through seemed like the best course of action to me too, and I could see the reasoning behind making the crossing at night. The problem was, I found the thought of travelling through the cold, dark night unsettling. I looked around at the snow falling beyond the trees we were lunching under.

"We should get back to it."

"The dogs are back, and they're closer," said Sarah, tugging on my sleeve and pointing back the way we had come.

I looked over my shoulder and felt the hair on the back of my neck rise. They were closer all right.

"Everybody on their bikes, let's go. Now!" I said.

My bicycle tire slipped in the slushy covering that was beginning to form over the road for the first few turns of my pedals, but then it caught and the bike shot forward. I tucked in as a back marker behind the others, Luke in front followed by Sarah and then the twins.

I didn't need to look over my shoulders to tell the dogs were coming, the sound of their baying told me all I needed to know. They weren't keeping their distance – this time they were chasing us down.

We rode as fast as we could under the circumstances, our bikes slipping and skidding on the icy road, but it was clear that we weren't going to outrun them. We would run out of steam long before the desperate canines did – either that or one of us would end up skidding off the road and be at the mercy of the pack.

I desperately looked around for some way out and spotted a large house ahead about fifty yards away. It wasn't set as far back from the road as most of the houses around it and the short gravel driveway was mostly clear of snow and slush.

Please don't be locked, the thought shot through my head so fast that I hardly had time to register it. I sped forward.

"There!" I shouted to the others and I pointed to the house. "Dump the bikes in the yard and get up on the porch!"

I angled dangerously off onto the driveway and jumped from the bike before it stopped. I hit the ground running, slipping in a patch of snow. I felt a sharp twang in my inner thigh as I did the splits before catching my balance.

The adrenalin running through me masked the pain and I scrambled up onto the porch, relieved to see that the others were all right there with me, adrenalin powering them all, even Sarah.

Ben rushed to the door and I turned, scrambling to pull my gun from my pocket as the dogs charged across the icy lawn.

It was Luke that saved us from what may have been a disaster.

With a guttural roar, he jumped off the porch, grabbed the shotgun from Ben's basket, and charged at the oncoming pack screaming like a maniac.

The sight of the crazy human was enough to cause some of the dogs to pull up and comically slide to a stop on the slippery grass. Three kept coming. Luke fired his shotgun at the pit bull that was leading the charge and it was flipped violently backwards by the blast.

The rest of the dogs scattered, frightened by the loud blast and the yelping of their pack mate. Luke paused and watched as the dogs ran off and then rakked the slide of the shotgun to load another round. He stepped up to the pit bull. It was still thrashing on the ground and yelping.

"Look away, everybody," he yelled.

I know the warning was mainly for the girls, but I also looked away too and watched as Ben tried to jimmy the door open. We all jumped as a second blast rang out and the agonized yips were abruptly silenced. When it was done, I turned around with my revolver in hand as Luke pulled a blanket from one of the packs and covered the dead dog before joining us on the porch.

Luke and I both watched the rest of the dogs with our guns ready. They had retreated to the road and had formed into a pack once again, watching us as warily as we watched them.

Behind us, Ben finally gave up trying to jimmy the door and attempted to ram it open with his shoulder. Sarah began tugging at the elbow of his parka. He shrugged her off and gave the door another ineffectual charge with his shoulder. Sarah didn't give up though.

Frustrated, Ben looked down at her.

"What?!"

She held up the shiny key she had pulled from under the corner of the welcome mat. Ben rubbed his shoulder sheepishly.

"Thanks," he mumbled, and took the key. With my adrenalin running high, I had to suppress a crazy, inappropriate (given what had just happened to the dog) giggle.

Luke and I stood guard as the rest piled inside. The dogs still milled aimlessly, sniffing the air in our direction, but hadn't worked up the courage to come back for more. I motioned Luke inside and without taking my eyes off the pack, I stepped in behind him.

The house was cold and there was no electricity or running water, or any sign that anybody had been there recently. Brooke made the mistake of opening the refrigerator door, discovering the moldering remains of a Christmas meal before slamming it closed again. Not before the smell escaped though.

"Brooke!" barked Ben, like a disappointed parent.

"Woops, sorry!" said Brooke and pulled a face behind his back, drawing a laugh from Sarah.

Luke started to up the stairs, but about halfway up encountered a smell that made the rotting food in the fridge smell like Potpourri. We didn't talk about what might be causing the stench, just agreed we would stay on the ground floor.

We all traipsed into the living room. One thing the place did have going for it was a big fireplace with a dozen or so logs sitting in the box next to it.

"Can we have a fire, Isaac, please?" Sarah asked.

"Tonight, maybe, when the smoke won't be as noticeable," I said. "That's if no one else objects."

"Sounds good to me, man," Luke said. "I feel like it's been ages since I've been really warm."

"I'm going to see if there is anything edible in this place," Ben said, moving toward the doorway to the kitchen.

"I'll help you," his sister said, following him.

"Should we get our stuff from the bikes?" Luke asked.

"The dogs are still out there," I said, peering through the aluminum venetian blinds.

They had finally gotten the gumption to come close to the house and were sniffing around their fallen pack mate. One of them, the big bristling Alsatian, sniffed at the dead pit bull, then bit into its leg.

A mutt approached and the Alsatian released the leg long enough to snap at him before chowing down again. Realizing there was food on offer, the rest of the dogs closed in and proceeded to scramble and fight over their former pack mate.

Feeling sick, I let the slats of the blind snap back into place.

"We'll have to wait," I said, not telling them what I'd just witnessed.

"Hopefully they don't get into our stuff."

"Yeah."

In the kitchen cupboards the twins found lots of canned food, including Irish Stew and baked beans and Campbell's soups. We all agreed that a few cans of Irish stew would make an excellent supper that night; frankly, we were all sick of baked beans in our supplies stack and knew they would be better cold than other foods while travelling.

We spent the remainder of the afternoon searching the ground floor of the big house for anything that would prove useful on our trip. Very little of what we found was actually suitable, although Sarah did uncover a box of small candy canes that we eagerly tore into.

Ben discovered an old boom box-style radio with working batteries in the kitchen and we turned it on. Running it through the FM dial, we expected to hear only static. We were shocked when we found a couple of the stations broadcasting.

Our rising hopes crashed when we realized that the stations were broadcasting in Chinese. Brooke, who had taken Mandarin in school for a year, said one was broadcasting in Mandarin and she wasn't sure about the other, although we figured it had to be Cantonese.

She was able to make out some of the words in the Mandarin broadcast, enough to tell that it was repeating the same few sentences over and over again but couldn't tell us what the message was.

"Sorry, I only took the subject because my mates did."

We flicked to AM stations, and after some frustration, we were able to find the coded message about the safe haven again, although it was now on a different frequency. Smart. It renewed my hope that if we did find this place, it would be well-organized and offer real safety. To my untrained ears, the series of beeps sounded the same as before, so after a while we shut it off.

"We should take the batteries when we leave, who can say when we'll come across more with juice in them," Luke said.

By then it was getting dark, so we decided to go ahead and light the fire. I wanted to wait until it was fully dark, but the others were impatient and the look of longing on Sarah's face melted my resistance.

We lit the fire just as dusk fell.

As the stew simmered over the fire, Sarah pulled out some old board games she had found under the sofa in the living room.

"We should play one," she said.

"What have you got there?" Luke asked.

"Let's see, Backgammon, Monopoly, Trouble and ... Chinese Checkers," she said, reading off the boxes.

We were all thinking it but, as usual, it was Luke who made the move. He picked up the Chinese Checkers box and tossed it onto the fire.

"Screw the Chinese!"

We watched silently as the flames licked the edge of the worn box before it caught alight and burned. It was a childish gesture of defiance, but somehow it made me feel better, and I could tell from the faces of the others that they felt the same.

"So, I guess it'll have to be Monopoly ... or Trouble, if one of us sits out," Brooke said.

"If you guys want to play Trouble, go ahead," I said. "I can watch the stew."

"No," Sarah shook her head. "We all have to play. Let's play Monopoly."

So that's what we did. It was like there was an unspoken agreement to give her everything she wanted that night.

We played, and talked, and laughed, and had fun, truly enjoying ourselves for the first time since we had all come together. For that few hours we managed to forget the horrors of the previous few weeks and simply be kids.

The stew was delicious after days of cold food and we all slept well that night, warm and comfortable in front of the fire. I wished we could have stayed there a few more days, or even permanently, but I knew that was not going to be possible.

Luke and I decided that we were going to have to move on the next morning and travel hard before we found a place to hole up for a few hours before making a night time dash across Worcester.

As I nodded off, I hoped that the dead pit bull had provided the pack with enough food to lose interest in us, otherwise our passage out of there and to the city would be even more dangerous.

After what happened the next morning, I stopped putting so much faith in hope.

15

I was in the kitchen gathering cans to take with us when it happened. A single piercing scream that transformed into shrieks of pain. I rushed into the living room, pulling my revolver from my pocket as I ran.

The front door was open and I burst through to find Sarah, surrounded by dogs on the lawn about near where we'd left the bikes. Luke was already on the porch with the shotgun in his hands, but I could tell he was hesitant to shoot for fear of hitting Sarah.

I brought the .38 up and pulled the trigger. It jumped in my hand as the report rang out. My aim was purposefully over the heads of the dogs and Sarah to scare them away; it didn't work. Some of the dogs shrank away but others continued tearing at her. Her bloodcurdling screams were muffled as she had been pushed face down into the snow by their assault.

At the sound of my shot, Luke's hesitation broke and he too leveled his gun, aiming at one of the dogs furthest away from Sarah. He squeezed the trigger and the shotgun boomed. The Alsatian pitched over and lay twitching in the snow.

The pack took more notice of us then, with all but one, a heavy American bulldog, forgetting Sarah and watching us warily, torn between food and self-preservation. The bulldog continued ripping at Sarah's shoulder and she screamed in agony.

I had a clean shot at a cadaverously thin Doberman and hit it in the head.

From behind me there was a shout and Ben rushed past us, charging at the dogs. He had the poker from the fireplace and swung it like a mad man.

"Bloody bastards! Leave her alone!"

The remaining dogs yelped and gave ground before him, but not quickly enough. Ben brought the bar of the poker down hard upon the muscled back of the bulldog and it squealed, turning to snarl at its attacker. Ben swung again, striking it on the side of its thick skull. It yelped before stumbling off in a weird drunken manner.

The last three dogs watched him just out of reach, their hackles raised, but not backing off. Ben picked Sarah up, hoisting her small, bleeding form over his shoulder.

He ran toward the porch with her and had almost made it when an emaciated mutt sank its teeth into the backside of his ski pants. Ben screamed in agony and dropped Sarah onto the steps, while swinging behind him with the poker in a desperate attempt to dislodge the dog's jaw.

Luke and I stepped forward at the same time. I grabbed Sarah under the arms and heaved her up onto the porch before picking her up. Just before I turned I saw Luke place the shotgun against the mutt's chest and pulled the trigger. The last of the dogs scattered, and I heard Luke firing off more shots as I took Sarah inside.

Placing Sarah gently in front of the fireplace, I looked her over as the others gathered around. She was unconscious, for which I was thankful. Her wounds were horrific.

Her right arm and shoulder were mangled, and she had multiple bites on her other arm and on both legs. She was bleeding profusely from the shoulder and, even as a 15-year old with no medical training, I knew that was not a good thing. Luke came in, helping Ben over to us; Ben was limping a little, white fluff protruding from the rips in his ski pants. He seemed to be angry rather than hurt.

Brooke stood frozen in the kitchen, her face pale with shock.

"Is she okay?" Luke asked.

"Does she look okay?" I snapped. "What the hell was she doing out there?"

"She went out to get something from her bike basket. I told her not to go, but she snuck out."

"We ... I ... said that we'd protect her," I said, as rage and anguish fought for control of my emotions, only realizing later that it was the first time I had felt those things since the death of my parents and sister. "Brooke, go to the bathroom, see if there are some clean towels. We need to try to stop the bleeding."

"I'm sorry I couldn't get to her faster, Isaac," Ben said, sitting awkwardly on a living room chair with his wounded backside half off the chair. "If I'd been faster maybe ..."

"No blame is going to be passed around here today," I said, my voice cracking. "We need to look out for each other, but we also all need to be responsible for ourselves."

"Fuck!"

It was the first time I had ever heard Luke use an obscenity stronger than 'crap' and I heard anguish, anger and, perhaps, regret in it.

We did what we could to staunch the bleeding and I made the call to build a fire in the fireplace to keep her warm. While it was dangerous to light a fire in the day, it seemed important to keep her comfortable.

Brooke sat with Sarah's head in her lap in front of the fire, while I pressed towels to the wounds. Brooke had also found some peroxide and I used it as a disinfectant. Luke disappeared and came back with an old power cord which he tried without much success to use as a tourniquet on her mangled shoulder.

We sat like that for an hour, changing the towels as they became soaked. Eventually Sarah stopped bleeding. I was relieved at first, until I realized that her chest wasn't moving.

Her pale face was as peaceful and calm as I'd ever seen it.

"At least she's stopped bleeding," Brooke said, using her finger to wipe a strand of hair from Sarah's brow. "Maybe now she can start getting better."

Luke, his face serious, looked at me and shook his head. I remembered a line from a book I'd read a long time ago: 'The dead don't bleed.'

Brooke continued to hold Sarah's head while I stood up and went to her brother.

Ben was standing at the front window, leaning against the sill and looking out at the bloody snow and dead dogs scattered over the ground.

"How are you doing?" I asked.

"I must say I've been better," Ben said with a grimace. "But after looking it over in the bathroom mirror, the bite on my bum isn't nearly as bad as it feels. I might be limping for a couple of days, but I'll live. Lucky I had jeans on under my snow pants; his teeth didn't break the skin, but it's pretty bruised." He looked at me, perhaps sensing that I wasn't only there to check up on him. "Sarah?"

"She's gone," I said quietly. "Brooke doesn't realize it yet, but she went a few minutes ago."

"Damn it," Ben said, shaking his head. "CPR? Shouldn't we try…?"

"It would've been no use. We couldn't stop the bleeding from her shoulder, it must have been an artery."

He looked like he wanted to cry.

"Poor Sarah … do you want me to talk to Brooke?"

"If you could, I just don't know what to say."

He nodded and pushed himself back from the wall.

"I can't say I know what to say either," he said and started limping to where his sister sat by the fireplace, still holding Sarah, and smoothing down her hair.

I walked out onto the front porch, hand on the revolver in my pocket in case the dogs had returned. They were nowhere to be seen. I didn't know what to do. Should we try to bury Sarah? Just leave her body behind? I walked down the porch steps and gave the stiffening body of the Doberman a kick to the side.

Tears spilled from my eyes, but this time rage won out and I began kicking the dead animal over and over, again and again, as I let out a muttered string of obscenities.

Finally, I sat down on the steps, breathing heavily, the tears now cold on my cheeks.

"Isaac?" Luke said from the doorway. "Isaac, I think we need to get out of here."

I wiped the tears from my face and stood up to look at him. He pointed into the sky without looking up and it was then I heard the faint rumble of a helicopter in the distance.

I looked up. The smoke from our chimney was rising, stark white against the slate gray sky.

"Quick, let's grab what we can and go," I said, springing into action. "We'll have to go on foot and try to stay in the trees."

Luckily, much of the land on either side of the road we'd followed to this point had been lightly forested.

"What about Sarah?" he asked, as I rushed to the bikes and started pulling out anything useful and light enough to carry on foot.

"We'll have to leave her here," I said, although the very thought of it pained me. "We can't take her with us and we don't have any time to bury her …"

"No. We can't leave her like that," he said, defiantly.

I paused and looked at him.

"How about we set the house alight and cremate her, so she isn't eaten by animals or left rotting like the people upstairs?" he suggested. "It might also distract the helicopter."

"Yes, yes, alright, do it quick while I get the others out."

Ben stood helplessly over Brooke as she held Sarah close, crying silently.

"We have to go, quickly!" I shouted. "The Chinese will be here soon."

Ben attempted to pull Brooke's hand, but she resisted and went back to stroking Sarah's hair. I ran to Ben and handed him the pack I'd hurriedly loaded.

"Go!"

I knelt beside Brooke and grasped her chin, gently tilting her face to meet my gaze.

"Brooke, Sarah's gone." I said. Looking in her eyes. "If we don't go now, right now, we'll be killed too."

The message seemed to get through and, still weeping, she slowly slid her legs out from under Sarah and eased her head onto the blanket.

"Hurry! They're getting closer!"

Ben, Brooke and I ran around like maniacs gathering what belongings we could as quickly as possible as Luke began splashing kerosene over the sitting room floor and furniture.

"Enough, go!" I yelled, stopping the twins after a minute. The choppers were too close.

Luke bent over Sarah and placed a sheet over her before kissing her shrouded forehead. That small heartfelt gesture was what amounted to her funeral and, as the noise of the chopper blades got louder, he poured kerosene over her before placing the tin to the side and striking a match. *Whump!* The fuel ignited and we ran out into the cold.

We hid in the cover of the trees a quarter mile away and watched the oily smoke rise into the sky as two helicopters circled like vultures over a carcass. Brooke's wracking sobs were the only sound that interrupted the heavy chop, chop, chop of the rotor blades.

16

The bare, dead branches of the deciduous trees, the most common in that area, didn't provide much cover, but luckily we had found a copse of spruce trees to crouch under as we watched. Thankfully, the helicopters didn't land and after ten or so minutes, they finished circling and departed.

"Great idea to set the house alight, Luke," said Ben. "I think maybe it worked as a decoy. I'm pretty sure if we'd only left the chimney burning, they would have landed and searched the area. We'd have been toast."

"Yeah, good thinking on your feet, Luke," I said, and patted his shoulder awkwardly.

"Well, it wasn't really about creating a decoy. I just didn't want to leave Sarah like that," he said.

Ben and I nodded somberly, but Brooke, still upset at the loss of the little girl, went to Luke and kissed him on the cheek. I heard her whisper, "Thank you."

Luke's eyes widened and I'm sure I saw a tinge of pink in his cheeks that hadn't been there a few moments ago.

"Shame about the supplies," he said awkwardly, bending over and picking up a backpack to distract us (or himself) from the moment.

We'd been forced to leave most of the supplies that we'd brought from Walmart; basically, all we had now was what we were wearing and what we had in our backpacks. I had gathered what I could from the baskets that the dogs had scattered, but it amounted to no more than some canned food and two sleeping bags.

"We should keep moving," I said, when the sound of the choppers had faded completely.

"Should we go back and gather up more supplies?" Ben asked.

"I don't think so," I replied. "They've scanned the area from the air but we have to assume they might send a patrol to search the area."

"I'll bet they do," Luke said. "And they'll probably be here sooner rather than later."

"Onward it is, then," Brooke said, looking sadly back in the direction of the house.

"We should stay off the road for a while," I said. "Luke, do you think you can guide us with the atlas and the compass you grabbed from Walmart?"

"Does a bear shit in the woods?"

His smile faded as his attempt to be light-hearted tanked; the death of Sarah was still too raw for all of us.

"Let's go, maybe we can find someplace closer to Worcester to hole up," I said quickly to cover the awkward silence.

After consulting his compass, Luke pointed us in a direction and we started our hike. The terrain rose slightly in that direction and the forest got thicker as we went on, despite the bare trees providing less cover than we would have liked.

The going was slow, and not just because of the terrain.

Both Ben and I were somewhat hobbled by our recent injuries, he the dog bite to the buttock, and me the pulled muscle in my groin from my dismount in the slushy snow.

It had been okay while I was warm, but this morning it was quite tender and the snow on the ground certainly didn't help. Nor the unevenness of the forest floor. As a result, we travelled much slower through the woods than we would have been along the road.

We'd been walking about twenty minutes when Luke stopped and looked worriedly behind us.

"What is it?" I asked.

"The snow," he said. "If somebody finds our trail in it leading away from the house, they can follow it right to us."

"Crap," I got a sinking feeling in my belly. "Well, let's push on, maybe we'll find a way ahead that'll confuse the trail. Besides we don't know that they actually will send a ground team. We just couldn't take the risk by hanging around."

"There should be a road on the top of this ridge, it runs the same direction as the one we were on," Luke said. "Maybe we can walk on it for a while before heading off into the woods again. At least it might slow them down if they're searching for our trail."

We walked on in silence for a good twenty more minutes before we came to the edge of the trees. We found ourselves looking into the backyard of a large house with a small barn-like building off to one side.

We scoped it for a few minutes but detected no signs of movement.

"Should we risk a quick pop inside to check for supplies, do you think?" Ben asked.

"If they do find our trail, I think it's too soon to stop, even for a short time," Luke said.

"Luke's right, we keep moving for now," I said, massaging my inner thigh as I crouched in the snow. "There'll be other houses to search once we're further away."

It started snowing again as we crossed the home's backyard, aiming for the gap between it and the barn. The snow was heavier than it had been before and if we still had them, riding the bicycles would have been a nightmare, or impossible.

On foot though, it wouldn't slow us down much more than what was already on the ground. This time, I was glad to see the snow falling – it was a light fall, but if it fell long enough, it would cover our tracks.

At the corner of the house, we found a large paved driveway that stretched off between the trees. A snow-covered SUV sat on the icy tarmac with its driver's side door open. I approached it warily. It was abandoned, and snow had begun to collect on the driver's seat.

"Follow the driveway," Luke said. "It'll be harder for somebody to follow our trail there because it's more slush and ice than snow."

The driveway was a couple hundred feet long and we followed it until it came out on another road at the rear of the property. Standing in the shadow of a large evergreen tree, we looked left and right. In both directions driveways led back to houses on either side of the street, most of them closer to the road than the one we had negotiated.

"I say we hang a left," Luke said. "It'll confuse followers because it sort of cuts back against the direction we've been going and, if I remember the map right, not too much further on there's a road we can take to put us back on course for Worcester."

"I've got a bad feeling about this road," I said.

I'm not sure what it was. The quiet seclusion of it, maybe? I was probably just spooked, but either way it just felt wrong.

Whether I was right or not, I had no intention of testing the theory.

"I think we should head straight across, through the backyard of the house across the way and back into the trees. It looks like there might be more evergreens over that way, so maybe that will make us harder to track if there is more snow in the branches and less on the ground."

"I agree with Isaac," Brooke said. "I don't like the idea of cutting back. I know it sounds clever, but it might just be too clever, if you take my meaning."

"In any case, let's do something," Ben said. "It's colder just standing around than it is walking."

"I guess I'm overruled," Luke said, with a smile. "Across and back into the woods it is."

We jogged across the road as best we could and then up a driveway on the far side. The snow was really starting to come down in thick, wet flakes and we hurried past the house and through the backyard, veering slightly to put the house between us and the road.

We came to a halt in front of a six-foot-high chain link fence that separated the backyard from the woods beyond.

"Up and over?" Luke asked.

"I'm not sure I can make it," I said with a wince as I thought of my aching inner thigh.

"Don't be a wuss, man," he said. "We'll help you."

Scrambling over the fence turned out to be far easier than I had feared it would be, no doubt because I had two other guys to help lift me, and we were soon back under the trees. There were more evergreens in this section of forest, which meant the ground was clearer and that less snow was falling on us from above. Luke used his compass to keep our course running north east, the direction he figured that we needed to go. The going was still slow, but we were making steady progress and I was even beginning to lose my fear that we might be tracked.

Twenty minutes later, we reached a road running roughly east to west and stopped so Luke could check his atlas. I checked my watch; it was a quarter after one, which meant that sunset would be in just over three hours.

"I know you want to avoid the roads," Luke said. "But we'd really make better time by following them."

"Yeah, I know," I replied. "We can follow this road for a while if you want, but we have to keep a good lookout. Last thing we want is a patrol catching us unaware."

"Thank the Almighty," Ben muttered.

In reality, I was nearly as relieved as him. The uneven ground of the forest floor, not to mention scrambling to step over fallen logs and forcing my way through bushes and brambles, had really upped the pain level in the muscle I had pulled.

"I think this road is this one here," Luke said, pointing at his map. "It goes from Northbridge back to the Worcester-Providence Turnpike. If we follow it to the left a bit, we should come to a road that branches off north east. Following that is a straight shot, well straight-ish at least, up to Millbury, which is just outside of Worcester, here." His finger traced a line on the map.

"How far are we from Millbury?" I asked.

"About two miles, as the crow flies, but probably closer to four following the roads with their twists and turns."

"About two hours hard walking then," said Brooke, tossing a glance at both her brother and I. "Assuming that you two don't collapse on us."

"I think I got another couple of hours in me," Ben said.

"Me too," I said, with much more conviction than I felt.

The snow was still falling, but at least there wasn't much wind as we began our trek to Millbury. Following the roads, we saw no signs of others, no adult survivors, no kids trying to survive on their own, no Chinese patrols looking for anybody, nothing. The world seemed so empty and peaceful. No planes in the sky, no cars on the roads, no sounds of construction or television. I could almost imagine what it must have been like for the pilgrims when they first landed on this vast, new continent.

Mr. Dresden in American History had told us that just a short while before Europeans arrived, there had been a large and thriving native culture, not only on the East coast of North America, but stretching nearly to the Rocky Mountains. The only reason that the continent had seemed so empty to the Europeans and that they'd encountered so few Native Americans was because a plague had swept through, killing off the majority.

While nature had conspired to give the Europeans a continent ripe for conquering and colonization, it seemed that the Chinese had taken matters into their own hands.

"Where do you suppose all of the kids are?" asked Luke quietly. "I mean, we've seen hardly any ... there's no way the Chinese could have rounded up more than a fraction."

I shrugged. I had been wondering that myself but hadn't liked the answers that had sprung to mind.

"Well, it's winter, there's no power or water, no adult supervision, no fresh food," I lowered my voice, so Brooke wouldn't hear. "I think a lot would be dead already. In this region, at least. It might be different in some of the warmer states, but then there are probably more Chinese there for that reason. They had to know that the cold would kill a lot of us."

"Maybe the dead are the lucky ones," Luke muttered, kicking at the snow.

17

The snow, coupled with Ben's injury and my own, meant that we still hadn't made it to Millbury when the sun started to descend beneath the horizon.

"We're about to pass by a town named Wilkersonville," Luke informed us, as we walked past a cemetery with the name 'St. Johns' above the gate. "We're still at least a mile from Millbury though."

"We should find someplace for the night," I said. "There is no way we'll be able to make Millbury before it gets dark."

"Yes, I agree," Ben said. His limp had grown more pronounced in the last half-hour or so.

Five minutes after we passed the cemetery, we approached a house sitting well back from the road on a half-acre of land. It was big and well-kept, and, I have to say, looked inviting in the bright twilight.

"That looks as good a place as any, don't you think?" asked Ben.

We all agreed it would be a good place to bed down for the night, so we turned to trudge up the long driveway.

We were about thirty feet from the front porch when the door opened, revealing a warm, yellow light within. Shocked, we all froze in place. My hand crept toward my pocket, and I only relaxed slightly when I saw it was a blonde-haired boy about our age or possibly a year or two younger. He looked around quickly and urgently gestured for us to come inside.

Whether it was the cold or the pain or the fatigue, I'm not sure, but we rushed as one toward the door without thinking about it.

The boy stepped aside quickly, allowing us to pile in and slammed the door behind us, shooting three large bolts home to secure the heavy door. We came to a standstill, panting and catching our breath as we found ourselves face to face with three more teenagers. These ones armed.

I felt my heart sink as Luke and the others put their hands up. I nearly pulled my .38 but thought better of it when I saw one of them was pointing a crossbow at Brooke's chest. The other two had a baseball bat and a machete, respectively.

I took my hand out of my pocket and raised my hands, praying that none of the others would do anything rash.

"Hey, sorry to rush you in like that, but we couldn't take the chance of you drawing attention to us," said the boy who had beckoned us into the house … or trap.

The blonde boy came around and gestured to his mates who lowered their weapons. He looked surer of himself now, and I reevaluated my first impression of him. Close up, I could see that he was probably my age; not only that, he appeared self-confident and was clearly the leader of their group.

"I'm Will; this is Beau, Ryan, and Rodney. Who's in charge of your little group?"

Luke gestured toward me.

"Isaac is. I'm Luke, and this is Ben and Brooke."

The twins nodded, still looking wary. Will smiled at them almost dismissively, his stare honing in on me. He appeared to be sizing me up. I stared back, not dropping my own gaze. I don't quite know what it was about him, the blonde good looks or his crooked smile, but I felt an instant mistrust.

Finally, he nodded and held out his hand and after a moment I shook it.

"Hey."

Formalities over, he pointed to a corner of the room.

"Please, make yourselves at home. You can put your stuff in that corner if you want. And you must be hungry? We were just about to eat."

"I could eat a horse and chase the jockey," said Luke, drawing a laugh from everyone except me.

Ben and Brooke also seemed to relax and joined Luke offloading their gear in the corner, Ben's backpack with the handle of the shotgun protruding in plain sight. If William and his friends noticed, they didn't let on.

Luke took his crossbow from his shoulder and placed it with his pack. Not quite convinced we were in no danger, I kept my jacket on and placed my backpack in the corner on top of Luke's weapon.

Now I had time to look around. We stood in a richly furnished parlor. The yellow light was coming from gas lanterns located at various points around the room and the toasty warmth immediately evident when we had come in was coming from a gas radiator.

The windows were blacked out by black plastic that hung behind the white lace curtains, effectively hiding the light of the lanterns to the outside. Ben and Brooke followed Will out of the room and Luke looked at me. I half expected him to tell me he was also wary of the occupants of the house, but instead he clapped me on the shoulder.

"Cheer up, Isaac! It smells like hot food!"

He was smiling ear to ear as he propelled me toward the door of what I could see was a dining room. I didn't like the way the other three boys hung back and waited us to go through.

I especially didn't like that they hadn't put their weapons down.

I looked back at them and saw the stockiest of the boys, the one carrying the crossbow, Beau, I think, stay behind and settle into a chair by the window. He pulled the dark plastic that was over the window to the side and peered out into the rapidly darkening afternoon.

"Beau's our lookout for tonight," said William, from directly behind me.

The large dining room opened into a kitchen that was also well-lit and invitingly warm. My mouth dropped open. All the available floor and bench space in the kitchen was taken up by canned and packaged food, and against one wall stood a stack of gallon containers of fresh water. On the gas stove, a large, probably industrial, kitchen-sized stock pot steamed happily.

I knew instantly it was the source of the wonderful meaty smell that made my stomach rumble despite my uneasiness. Will informed us it was beef stew and invited us to sit at the huge table that dominated the space.

"Ryan, set our guests a place please. Rodney, you can start to serve."

Rodney and Ryan put their weapons on the kitchen counter and got busy.

Within a few minutes we were at the table, as Rodney, a big sullen boy, went from place to place ladling stew into our bowls. I took in the empty chair next to Brooke and an image of Sarah flashed across my mind. It was hard to believe that just 24 hours before we had been laughing and enjoying our game of Monopoly with her.

She should have been here too.

Rodney was just serving Ben, the last of us to have his bowl filled with the delicious smelling stew, when Will clapped his hands suddenly. Entranced by the aroma and ready to dig in as we were, we all jumped.

"I almost forgot!"

We watched him scoot around the counter to the oven. A second later he returned carrying a wooden board with two huge loaves of freshly baked bread. Luke and the twins greeted this unexpected sight with shouts of pleasure.

I was silent, but my mouth watered in anticipation. After surviving so long on canned, mostly cold food, the feast laid before us seemed to be Heaven sent. As excited at the prospect of a warm meal as I was, the oddness of these boys picked at the edges of my consciousness.

William seemed content, almost happy, for us to make pigs of ourselves. There was plenty to go around and they clearly weren't wanting. We broke the bread off in chunks and dipped it into the generous bowls of the tasty stew.

I slowly relaxed as we ate. The hearty food and the buoyant mood of my group gradually chipped away at my disquiet. Will was quite the host and I didn't fail to notice that Brooke appeared to be quite smitten with him, laughing enthusiastically at his jokes and stories. This didn't seem to bother Luke or Ben who were as engaged as she was by our charismatic host.

It turned out that Will's group had made several raids into Millbury, one time managing to start an old truck and load it with all the supplies they could fit. I told them the story of the pickup and the dreadful aerial response from the Chinese.

Will shrugged.

"Luckily, it was only a short journey for us."

My disquiet again reared its ugly head. Not only because of the lack of detail he provided to explain their good fortune, but also at the lack of conversation from the other boys. It was almost as if they had been ordered not to speak.

After dinner Will showed us where we could clean up, a small bathroom down the hall from the kitchen, and then invited us back into the parlor. We fell to the carpet around the radiator, our full bellies bulging.

Beau still sat at the window, barely acknowledging the rest of us as we came in. He clearly took his job as a sentry very seriously.

"Have you had much trouble?" I asked, addressing him.

He just looked at me like I'd spoken a foreign tongue.

I saw Rodney, who was standing in the doorway to the dining room, give Will a strange look that none of the others saw.

"Honestly, we've been really lucky," Will answered for him. "Like you, we've had some looters come through, but each time we've been able to scare them off. There was also a group of about twelve kids; we put them up for a couple of nights before they moved on."

This last comment piqued my interest.

"Where did they move on to?"

"Um ... they were heading to the city," he said.

"Worcester?" Luke asked.

"Yes," he said quickly. "What about you all? What are your plans?"

Before I could say anything, Brooke had blurted about New Hampshire and the Morse code signal. I felt a flash of anger but held my tongue. William was silent for a moment, digesting this information. I think he was about to ask more questions when she followed up with an enthusiastic, "You should come with us!"

"Thanks for the offer, but we're happy here. Well, for the winter at least. You're welcome to stay tonight though ... for as long as you want," he replied, graciously. I breathed an inward sigh of relief, both at his refusal and the offer of a night's accommodation.

"Oh, marvelous! Thank you, Will, you're very kind," said Brooke. She turned to me. "Can we stay Isaac?"

"Yes, it sounds like a great idea to get our strength back. I vote for staying a few days," said Ben.

"Me too, Boss," said Luke.

"Thanks for the offer," I said, outnumbered but resolute. "We'll take you up on tonight, but only one night. We'll leave in the morning."

"It makes sense to stay at least another night, Isaac," Will said, almost too quickly. "To gather your strength ... and to be honest," he smiled at Brooke, "we really could do with the company."

Ben and Brooke enthusiastically backed him up, but Luke for the first time wasn't quite as keen – I'm pretty sure it had something to do with that look he'd seen Will give Brooke. Put on the spot, I couldn't come up with a reason to say no outright so I did the next best thing.

"Alright, we'll stay tonight, and make our decision about tomorrow night after breakfast."

"Sounds good," said Luke, offering me a knuckle bump.

Ben and Brooke weren't quite satisfied with that decision but didn't argue. Yet.

We didn't chat much longer; our group was bushed after our flight from the last refuge. Will ordered Rodney to bring mattresses and pillows to the parlor. It seemed odd, this smaller boy ordering the bigger one about like that, but Rodney took it with no complaint.

Will bid us goodnight and went to his own bedroom, which was apparently one of the perks of being in charge. Ten minutes later, the twins were asleep on a double mattress and Luke had taken a comfortable looking sofa and was snoring softly.

I was on a single mattress, watching the comings and goings of Will's group and attempting to ward off sleep. Ryan had relieved Beau at the window, and Beau was also now quietly snoring in an armchair. Rodney had disappeared with Will.

A tide of weariness lapped at the beach of my consciousness and I closed my eyes, telling myself it would just be for a second. My sleep was fitful at first and I remember jumping a few times. One of those times, I saw Ryan at the window, cradling the crossbow as he regarded me with his expressionless, pale face. He looked away immediately and I slowly relaxed.

Soon I fell into a deep, dreamless sleep.

I awoke late the next morning, alone in the room except for Rodney who at some point had relieved Ryan at the window. I chastised myself. I had slept in after everyone again, not even stirring when they had gotten up. I'd read about soldiers being able to sleep at any time and waking up at the slightest noise. I wondered how long I had to live in this new world of almost constant danger before I would be able to do that.

"Where are the others?" I asked Rodney.

"Out back," he said, without looking at me.

I stood up and picked up the jacket I had curled into a ball and used as a pillow. I felt the comforting shape of the .38 and then put the jacket on carefully so as not to drop it. There were plates on the table in the kitchen with the remains of a pancake breakfast on them. That's not what caught my attention though – it was the laughing and squeals of delight from outside.

I went to the sliding door; its glass had been taped and blacked out too. I peeked through a crack and was surprised to see Ben, Brooke, Luke, and the rest of our hosts running around like lunatics throwing snowballs at each other.

They were in a private courtyard bordered by a tall hedge. As I watched, Luke failed to duck a fastball from Will and fell on his butt, his face covered in ice. I couldn't help but smile and slid open the door.

"Hello, sleepyhead!" yelled Brooke, running up to me and giving me a hug as I stepped out. Her cheeks were pink, and her eyes watery, and she looked just about the happiest I had ever seen her.

Whether my presence was a dampener, or the game had come to a natural conclusion, I don't know, but we headed back inside almost immediately and Will made us mugs of hot chocolate using powdered milk and cocoa. I accepted the last two pancakes, and even though they were cold, they were delicious.

Will fell into a conversation with the others about the before times and I excused myself. I needed to whiz badly and walked down the hall to the bathroom Will had pointed out the night before.

I had my hand on the door handle when I decided to have a quick peek in one of the other rooms. This was the first time I'd been alone without one of their group within sight.

The door swung open on silent hinges and I found myself looking into what used to be a child's bedroom. I whistled softly. The room's pink walls were stacked high with cardboard boxes of food. Powdered milk, flour, dehydrated eggs, canned vegetables, and more water.

Suddenly, Will's explanation of raids on the local supermarket seemed weak at best; this stuff looked like it had been taken from a warehouse. Fair enough if they'd found a goldmine and didn't want to share, but I didn't like being lied to. I closed the door. As I relieved myself, I was even more convinced that we should leave first thing in the morning tomorrow. I knew there was zero chance of persuading the others to go today; I'd left my run too late.

The rest of the day passed uneventfully with board games and some cards and after another hearty meal, we discussed our plans for the morning. Rodney, who would be on watch that night, was to awaken us just before daybreak so we could resume our journey. Brooke and Ben tried to persuade me that we should stay longer, but with Luke's support I won out.

Will didn't try talking us into staying longer this time. We soon found out why.

18

The crash of the front door being kicked open ripped me from sleep and I sat up fast. Red beams of light cut through the darkness of the parlor as a handful of figures rushed through the front door shouting in Chinese.

Instantly alert, I dug through my jacket for my handgun. It was gone.

In the glow of the weapons a figure loomed over me and I looked up to see Will's smiling face.

"What the hell ..." I began to scramble to my feet and immediately found myself back on the floor with my cheek stinging. The little weasel had slapped me across the face.

Confused and enraged, I tried to rise to my feet again, only to feel a cold, hard ring of metal pressed against my neck.

I froze and in the wildly changing backdrop of shadows and light, I saw the gangly silhouette of Luke tackle another stocky form, probably Rodney, and shoot back to his feet with the baseball bat in his hand.

Luke's back was to me and I saw him wind up, preparing to club the nearest interloper. He didn't finish his swing. A series of three loud bangs, each accompanied by a bright flash, sounded from the direction of the door.

I saw Luke jerk as each of the bullets hit him.

"No!" I screamed helplessly, as he fell with a heavy thud.

There was a voice yelling in Chinese near the door to the dining room.

"Stay the bloody hell away from my sister!" yelled Ben, before groaning in pain.

I pulled myself up, ignoring the weapon pressed against my neck and ran to the prone figure of Luke. I hadn't made it three feet when there was a loud pop and something that felt like a speeding bus hit my right arm and shoulder, sending me spinning to the floor.

I've been shot!

The thought reverberated through my mind as I lay winded, trying to get my breath back. I reached over and ran my left hand up my right arm to the shoulder.

I didn't feel any blood, but my entire upper arm and shoulder were numb. What the hell? Then the answer came to me. Rubber bullets, like the ones police use in riots. Relief washed over me. Luke wasn't dead.

Someone shouted in Chinese again, closer this time, and I was pulled roughly to my feet. One of the lanterns was lit and I turned to look, my eyes swimming with tears of pain and frustration.

Will approached one of the Chinese soldiers. By the light of the lantern, I saw the soldiers were all clad in black and carrying strange, large barreled guns. The treacherous bastard handed my pistol and Luke's crossbow to one of them, then turned and approached me, smiling.

"You won't be needing those anymore."

Fury engulfed me, and I broke free of the soldier holding my arm and hammered Will square on the nose with a beautiful right hook. His nose crunched under my fist and gushed technicolor red as he fell backwards with a groan.

I stood over him waiting, almost praying, for him to get back up. A hand turned me and a Chinese rifle butt caught me dead center in the forehead.

The world went dark.

Part Three

ENCOUNTERS

19

I don't know how long I was out, but when I awoke, I was lying face down on a cold, unyielding surface that was bouncing and vibrating under me. I hurt. My right arm and shoulder felt like they were about to fall off and my head was splitting agony.

My arms were behind my back and I felt a tight pressure around my wrists. After a few moments, I became aware of the noises around me including the noise of an engine. I was in a truck or van. I began to struggle, which caused the bindings on my wrists to feel as if they were cutting into my skin.

"It'll be alright," I heard a voice whisper.

Ben.

"Shush, we don't want the guards back here again," I heard Brooke whisper back.

Turning my head in their direction, I strained my eyes to try and see anything in the darkness. It was pitch black, wherever we were. I gave up and just closed my eyes again.

"What happened to Luke?" I asked, speaking as loudly as I dared, which is to say a harsh whisper.

"Isaac, you're awake?" said Ben, relief flooding his voice. "We've been captured by a Chinese patrol."

"Thanks for the news flash, old chap," I said, then groaned as I rolled over toward their voices.

"Luke's in here too, someplace, probably still unconscious from his last thrashing," he responded evenly, my sarcasm lost on him or ignored.

"Be quieter, both of you," Brooke said, under her breath. "Luke woke up when they were loading us into the back and he made a ruckus. They hit him on the back of the neck and knocked him out again. We wouldn't want the same thing to happen to any of us."

"Any idea where we are or where they're taking us?" I asked, dropping my whisper lower.

"No, they tied our hands behind our backs and piled us into the back of this lorry ... truck," Ben explained. "I tried to catch what they were saying to those traitors, but they were too far away. You really got that little prick a good one by the way. I imagine he'll think twice before he mouths off to someone again."

Will ... yes, it all made sense now, the abundant food, the gas, and the insistence we stay just one more night. Their strange willingness to help us. They were working for the Chinese, trapping unsuspecting American kids and calling them in to collect. The house was a honey trap.

"How long was I out?"

"We've been driving for about 30 minutes."

Thirty minutes? Was that all? I felt like I had been out for a whole day, at least. I tried to sit up, which was not easy with my hands tied behind my back. Finally, I shuffled to the wall of the truck and managed to maneuver myself into a sitting position.

Twisting my hands and fingers around, I discovered thin plastic bindings held my wrists. They had not actually cut into me but were tight enough that my fingers were starting to get tingly.

"What are we going to do Isaac?" Ben asked.

I felt helpless and very much lacking as a leader right then, even though I hadn't asked for the gig.

"I'm not sure, let me think on it for a while."

We fell into silence. To be honest, I didn't do a whole lot of thinking. The pain in my head and the other injuries I'd suffered didn't leave room for much besides self-pity. About a half-hour after I awoke, a groan came from the darkness near the rear of the truck.

"Luke?"

"Yeah," he groaned. "I think my skull is caved in. Where are we?"

"Still in the truck, don't speak too loudly."

"Yeah, not sure I could if I wanted to … Ben and Brooke?"

"We're here," the twins said in uncanny unison.

Luke giggled despite his obvious pain.

"Just rest for now," I said. "Not much else we can do."

"Okay."

We fell silent again. I still felt disoriented but was slowly coming back to my senses. The truck drove on at an even speed, slowing occasionally to turn in tight arcs before speeding up again. Weaving past abandoned vehicles, I assumed.

After what I think was about another half-hour, the vehicle slowed, and I found myself sliding across the metal floor and tipping onto my right side as the driver turned the corner a little too fast. I barely registered the truck stopping through the reignited pain in my bruised arm and shoulder.

Doors slammed up front and there was a short pause before the roller door clattered open to reveal the silhouettes of our captors. I blinked rapidly as my eyes adjusted to the dim light. One of the soldiers climbed in.

"Pit stop," he said, in heavily accented, but surprisingly good English. "You will use the bathroom now."

We learned later that many Chinese patrols had soldiers attached to their units who had spent time in America as exchange students.

"What if we don't have to go?" Luke groaned.

"It's your last chance to go. We have a long drive ahead and no more pit stops. The only stops ahead are to collect more kids like you along the way."

"I could take a leak," I said, using the wall to force myself to my feet. "Thanks."

"You are all going, everybody up. And no funny stuff; we're watching, and we've put away the rubber bullets from last night. If you try to run, we'll use the real thing," the soldier said, patting the small machine gun he was holding before slinging it over his shoulder.

The rubber bullets had been bad enough; I never wanted to feel the impact of a live round, that was for sure. I stepped down out from the van with the help of the English-speaking soldier. We were at a rest stop beside a freeway and it was still dark, but the sky was brightening with a pink, pre-dawn glow.

At the restroom door, the soldier stopped us.

"One at a time," he said. "I am watching, and Chan is watching around the back. Like I said, no funny stuff."

He pulled Brooke forward and turned her around, pulling a small pocketknife from the pocket of his uniform. He cut through the zip-tie with one movement and shoved her toward the door.

"Ladies first," he said.

Brooke disappeared inside, but not before giving him a defiant stare over her shoulder.

"You and Chan, huh? How many more of you bastards are there?" asked Luke.

My eyes widened.

The soldier looked at Luke, his cheekbone and chin bruised from his previous beating, and smiled dangerously. Without warning, he delivered a hard slap across his face.

Luke looked at him insolently.

"You have already been more trouble than you are worth, Mr. Redhead," the soldier said. "You'd better hope we don't find many more pick-ups between here and Washington. If the truck gets too full, it's possible that accidents may happen to some of you."

"Washington state or the city?" I asked quickly.

My reason for the question was to take his attention from Luke, who looked like he was about to do some more poking. It was risky asking questions, but no riskier than Luke getting killed for impertinence.

The soldier turned his gaze on me.

"We think it is important to take you to a work camp in an unfamiliar area," he said. "Less chance of trouble. But trucking you all the way across the country is cost prohibitive. New workers are relocated north and south, not east and west."

"The city then," I replied, surprised that he was happy to talk.

"Yes," he said. "The city."

"You speak English very well," I said. "Where did you learn it?"

"Stanford," he said. "I went to graduate school there. American graduate schools are a joke. Or were..."

"You have an advanced degree?" I asked. "What are you doing on a detail like this?"

"Like I said, American graduate schools were a joke. Most businesses and government agencies at home consider my Doctorate in Anthropology to be little better than the Chinese equivalent of a master's degree." The soldier stepped over to the restroom door and rapped loudly. "You are taking a long time, honey. Hurry up!"

It was then, over his shoulder, that my eyes were drawn to the shadows at the corner of the bathroom block. At first, I thought I was hallucinating, but when I concentrated there was no doubt. Someone in a ski mask, their head a darker shape in the shadows, was peering at us from the corner of the building.

I didn't react. I was pretty sure the others didn't spot our visitor, and the arrogant soldier was oblivious.

Then the shape was gone, vanishing so quickly I almost questioned whether I had really seen anything.

"You have until I count to three," the soldier yelled and banged on the door. "After that, if I must, I will come in and help you finish up."

"You bloody ..." Ben started, but Luke and I quickly stepped between him and the soldier.

"That won't help, Ben," I said, for the benefit of our captor, then mouthed *just wait* before: "It'll just get you beaten up like us."

Ben and Luke looked at me with eyebrows raised but we all turned to the soldier when he began to count.

"One ... two ... thr-"

He didn't finish his count. We saw him tense and stiffen before stumbling away from the door and spinning around to look at us angrily. We stepped back as he reached over his shoulder grasping for something.

"What ...?" he began but crumpled to the ground before he could finish.

I rushed over to him and fell to my knees, twisting my back to him as I tried to put my hands close to the knife that hung on his belt.

"Quick, help me get his knife," I said to Luke. "We can cut our wrists free and get the hell out of here." I knew the person in black had done this, but I had no way of knowing if the enemy of my enemy was my friend. If we could get free and get the truck, we might not need to find out.

"Um, Isaac," Luke replied, looking over my shoulder and not moving.

"What are you waiting for Luke? Hurry!"

"Isaac, there are two guys dressed like Ninjas right behind you."

"Yes," said Ben, stepping up beside him. "And they aren't the turtle kind."

I spun around and saw the black clad person I had seen before and a taller man, dressed identically. They weren't really dressed as Ninjas, I realized; they were in black Kung Fu gear with ski masks. The taller one was holding a sort of tube thing in his hands and I realized it was a blowgun. My friend Tommy used to have the NERF version of one – we'd played with it the last time I had seen him.

"Cut them free," the taller figure said to his partner. "I'm going to go see if Allie and Arthur have secured the truck."

"This guard said there was another one around the back of the building," I said.

"Already taken care of, before we got your friend out through the bathroom window," our mysterious savior said as he walked away.

"Is Brooke safe?" Ben asked the one who approached us.

"The girl? Yes. Well, as safe as can be expected," he said, producing a pocket knife. "Turn around and I'll free your hands."

He quickly cut us free and pulled his mask off to reveal a teenage face framed by shaggy blond hair. With the ski-mask off, he looked more like a surfer than a Ninja.

"Thanks," I said. "I'm Isaac, this is Luke and Ben."

"I'm John," he replied. "Follow me. Sonny wants us to gather at the truck."

"What truck?" Luke asked.

"The one you came in of course. Come on."

We followed John back to the truck, where we found two more 'Ninjas'. They were standing over two more Chinese soldiers who were laid out next to the cab; both of their heads rested at awkward angles.

"Oh dear," Ben said, quietly.

As we reached them, the taller one, and a girl with long dark hair holding her ski mask in her hand, led Brooke out to us. The tall one, who was obviously the leader, then pulled off his mask.

He was Chinese.

I guess I flinched, because he looked at me and immediately burst out laughing.

"Don't freak out, man," he said in a perfect American accent, and held out his hand. "I'm not one of them, but luckily I have their genes or I'd have been dead meat when the Flu hit. I'm Sonny Li."

I shook his hand and introduced our group. Within a few minutes, we had our backpacks back, and, happily, also our weapons. They had been confiscated by the Chinese back at Will's and had been loaded into a cargo trunk under the side of the truck. Obviously, the Chinese didn't allow Will's group to keep more weapons than necessary.

Sonny offered us refuge with his group for as long as we wanted. Unlike my first impression of Will, Sonny came across as welcoming and honest from the get go and besides, he had demonstrated clearly that he wasn't in cahoots with the Chinese. They were based in Worcester too, which was our next goal, so we all agreed to take up their offer.

"You guys get the truck loaded, I have something to take care of. John, you can help me."

They headed back to the restrooms and when they returned, Sonny was wearing the uniform of the man who had been escorting us. The look on his face was grim and it didn't take much to work out what he'd done with the unconscious officer. From the rear of the truck where I was about to climb in, I saw them drag the two bodies by the truck away.

When they were done John climbed in with us and Sonny closed the roller door. The pit stop had come at the first rest area on the freeway between Worcester and Boston. Sonny's other 'ninjas' were all teenagers – Allie, Karen, and Arthur.

During the trip Sonny's crew were very forthcoming, and we asked a lot of questions.

It turned out Sonny was a Chinese-American, born in China less than a week before his parents had come to live in the United States. Sonny had no memories of his homeland. He barely spoke Chinese as his father had been adamant that he be raised as an American. The only place where this didn't apply was in martial arts. Mr. Li had made sure his son was well-trained in traditional Chinese arts, such as Tai Chi and Wing Chun Kung Fu.

Sonny had apparently taken such training to heart. The others explained he'd won several martial arts tournaments as a teen and young adult and, when the infection came, the 28-year old Sonny had been the sifu of one of the most popular martial arts academies in the state.

Arthur, John, Allie, and Karen were what remained of his students, along with Mark and Samara who had been left back at their base of operations. I didn't let on about my own Kung Fu experience just then. We had only just met them and as good as the first impressions were, I felt it might be better to keep my cards close to my chest, especially given what had happened when we trusted Will and his group.

After a quick stop at a department store outside of Worcester to load some supplies into the back of the truck, we were soon on our way to the martial arts academy where Sonny and his students had been holed up since Hell Week.

20

Sonny parked the truck in the underground garage next to the academy and we helped unload the supplies they'd picked up. The academy took up the whole ground floor of a low-rise building. It was carpeted and tidy, with equipment and gear stowed neatly on shelving against the wall. I also saw a rack of assorted hand weapons that took my interest.

When we were done, we sat around a table drinking long life apple juice Sonny had poured us as the others packed away the new supplies. I asked him if he'd felt safe driving the truck.

"They mark their trucks with a special paint on the top to identify them to their satellites, so until the truck is reported as overdue, Chinese monitoring won't pick up the truck as a threat. Of course, it's lucky they don't have checkpoints set up here yet. I'm not so confident I could have bluffed my way through a face to face meeting. Uniform or no uniform."

"Will you get rid of it?" asked Luke.

"Yeah, we can't keep it very long. Tonight after dark we'll drive it to a different parking garage and burn it," Sonny said. "This'll make the third truck we've hijakked from them in two weeks, so the heat might be on if they work out where we've ended up."

"Third?" I said. "And they haven't changed their routines or sent an armed response?"

"Just choppers. I think the first couple of times they probably thought it's just a group of kids. Might be different this time, given that there were prisoners in it and that we killed four soldiers instead of the two we were expecting. We have a radio from the soldier in the first truck we took, so we listen in on their chatter now and then, although I'm the only one here that even partially understands it."

"They're probably speaking Mandarin, while it sounds like you might be Cantonese," Brooke said.

"That's right, how did you know?" He looked impressed.

"They call you Sifu," Brooke said. "That's a Cantonese term. In Mandarin, the term is Shifu – subtle, but still a difference."

"You speak Chinese?" Sonny asked.

"Just a little," she replied, blushing. "I had a year of Mandarin, and the teacher often liked to point out the difference between Mandarin and Cantonese."

"Do you or any of your blokes know Morse code, by any chance?" Ben asked, stepping up beside his sister and placing a hand on her shoulder.

"I think Arthur and John have a handle on it," Sonny said. "They were both Boy Scouts. Why?"

We spent a half hour telling Sonny what we knew of the message and what we had worked out. I think we'd all just decided it had to be done. We had to trust someone, and this seemed like the right opportunity and the right company to do it in.

"Do you have a normal radio with AM reception?" I asked. "It would be great to get the message written down, so we have more to go on."

"Of course, although we haven't turned it on in weeks. I hadn't even thought of trying the AM channels," Sonny said, and pointed to Luke and me. "We'll get it out later. Let's check your injuries first, you two especially look like you've been in the wars."

Sonny, who apparently had some medical knowledge but no formal training, took some time to check over our assorted injuries and bruises. Brooke made herself scarce when Luke and I took off our shirts while Ben looked as if he was torn between mentioning his dog bite on the backside or following his sister out the door. In the end he chose the latter and Luke and I had a chuckle.

"Anything I should be aware of?" asked Sonny.

"No, nothing," I said, still smiling.

Sonny probed the lump on my forehead as gently as he could, but it hurt like hell. I sucked in a pained breath.

"Sorry. I don't think your skull is fractured, but you probably still have a mild concussion. The lump on your head and the black eyes will fade in a week or two."

My arm and shoulder had come out in a massive purple bruise where the rubber bullet had hit me, but again he didn't think there were any fractures or permanent damage.

At least the new injuries meant I barely even felt the muscle I had strained in my thigh anymore. He moved on to Luke. Luke's ribcage was badly bruised and based on the tenderness, Sonny thought he may have some cracked ribs.

"Of course, without an X-ray it's impossible to tell, but I'll strap you up anyway."

He didn't show any signs of concussion when Sonny looked into his eyes. Apparently, the Chinese soldiers had been quite skillful in disabling us without doing too much damage.

When he was done, he looked us over.

"You guys look beat and after what you went through, who can blame you? Go ahead and take a load off. The practice mats make excellent beds. I'll wake you if we learn anything new."

That is exactly what we did. The practice mats did make rather good mattresses to sleep on compared to the rocky ground, although they weren't really comparable to a real bed … beggars aren't choosers though. Ben and Brooke bunked down with us too and Sonny made sure the other kids gave us some time to ourselves.

Luke and Ben were snoring almost as soon as they lay down and Brooke was sleeping soundly not long after.

I was tired too, but it took a while for me to get to sleep. I was thinking about how lucky we had been. Lucky that our captors had chosen to stop where they had, lucky that Sonny and his group had been out that particular night on one of their 'missions' to harass the enemy.

Hopefully it meant our fortunes were turning.

I also thought about Sonny. He had been born in China, but raised as an American, and he had a rage inside of him that scared me a little when I heard him talk about the Chinese that were invading his 'homeland.'

He seemed competent at leading his group of students and, if the trophies in the case by the front doors of the academy were any indication, he was probably capable of kicking a tremendous amount of butt. I worried though, what would happen to him and his wards if the Chinese military decided to launch a strike on Worcester to stop the truck disappearances.

I did not want to be here when that went down.

A few isolated patrols without support were one thing, but somehow I doubted that Sonny's 'Ninjas' would be up to taking on a larger group of Chinese soldiers focused on hunting them down. I decided I would do my best to talk them into coming with us to the safe haven. They would certainly be an asset to our little group.

Finally, my weariness got the better of me and I fell asleep feeling more hopeful than I had since the dog attack. I rarely remember my dreams, but that day I clearly remember dreaming of Sarah on a road winding its way through a forest. She was walking away from me and wouldn't look back, no matter how loud I called or how far I followed her.

It was late afternoon before Sonny woke us up. He told us that both Arthur and John had listened to the coded message, and confirmed it was the same message repeated over and over, switching frequencies every other time.

"Maybe its automated? It might even be a trap?" he worried.

"Maybe, but I don't think the Chinese would go to all that trouble when they just round up everyone," said Luke. "They have all the time in the world, after all."

Excited, we all rushed to the kitchen where Arthur and John sat by the radio.

Arthur slid the writing pad to me.

Safe haven NH. Look for the dragon on the White Mount.

"So, there's no actual location? This isn't much more than we already knew," I said, slightly disappointed.

"No, it figures," said Luke. "They can't be too detailed; it has to be cryptic in case the Chinese come across it. I don't even know if they use Morse code, but if they do, the message is backwards and only contains clues. It's pretty clever, really. Let me get my atlas, now that we have light and my fingers aren't ice blocks."

He rushed out of the room.

"When we go, are you going to come with us?" I asked. "We'd be glad to have you."

Sonny didn't answer straight away, perhaps conscious of the stares from Arthur and John.

"I don't know," he said. "We have it pretty sweet here at the moment, but who knows how long that will last?"

"True. And think, even if we don't find any other survivors there, it's going to take the Chinese longer to colonize the mountains of New Hampshire than it is the urban centers like Worcester," I said.

He nodded, looking thoughtful.

"We'd have to think on it and run it by the others to see what they think."

Luke hustled back in, slamming the atlas on the table and pouring over the map of New Hampshire. I looked over his shoulder as he ran his finger over and around the part of the map showing the White Mountains National Forest. His finger halted after only 30 seconds, then he pressed it into the page hard enough for the tip to go white.

"There it is my friends!" he declared, looking at me triumphantly. He was pointing at a spot in the national park identified as 'Drake Mountain'.

"Drake Mountain?"

The others joined us, jostling for a view and bumping heads.

"Yes!" he said.

"Drake Mountain? What about it?"

"Drake! Drake is another word for dragon! Dragon on the white mount!"

"Ah, of course!" I said, the penny finally dropping.

"I've been there!" said a voice behind us. It was Allie, she had come into the room as we crowded over the map. "My parents took me to the Drake Mountain Ski Resort two years ago!"

"Well done, Luke!" said Sonny, clapping him on the shoulder.

My friend looked extremely happy with himself and I couldn't blame him. For the moment we were all happy, the woes of the world forgotten in the glow of this little beacon of hope.

After we had all calmed down a little, we talked through what we had found out.

"So, it's close to Lincoln, on the southern edge of the White Mountain National Forest," said Sonny. "That's about 150 miles from here to there. Not a fun trip and especially now that the weather looks like it's turning for the worse."

"He's right," Luke said, after a quick flip back to the Massachusetts' page. "That's a hell of a walk, man."

"I'm hoping we don't have to."

"To what?"

"Walk," I said with a smile. "Sonny's shown us the way. We commandeer a Chinese patrol truck and drive it there; 150 miles shouldn't take us longer than say, three or four hours? If we have any luck at all, we can do that well before it's reported overdue."

"I'm not sure I'd count on our luck, dude," Luke said, shaking his head. "It seems to be running both ways lately and there's no telling when it'll be good or bad."

21

Later, when we were alone, Luke and I ran through our options.

"We have a while to work on a plan," I said. "A few days at least, until the uproar over the missing truck dies down."

"Stay here in the meantime?"

"If Sonny will let us. He seems like a straight up guy," I said.

"I can deal with a few more nights sleeping on those mats," Luke said, his face splitting into a smile. "After the beatings and rubber bullets, my body needs a recharge."

"Yep, me too," I said.

A couple of hours later, as night began to fall, Sonny asked if any of us wanted to ride with him to dump the rental truck in a parking garage about a few blocks away. Arthur, Karen and I put our hands up.

Arthur and Karen were both about my age. She was a pretty redhead with, by all reports, a fiery temper. Arthur was tall and muscular, with a shock of brown hair and a nose like a knife blade. Despite their bickering over silly things like who would sit by the passenger side window, it was obvious to me they had a thing for each other.

We took along two five-gallon gas cans and a single 20-pound portable propane tank.

"Grab the propane and gas out of the back," Sonny said to Arthur as he parked the truck in the underground parking garage. We had gone down two levels below the street and parked in an area well clear of other vehicles and structures.

Arthur jumped to it and we soon had the propane canister sitting on the floor of the cab beneath the dashboard.

"Spread the gas in that can around the cargo area of the truck," Sonny instructed Karen, while Arthur dumped the contents of the other can in the cab, making sure to get a nice puddle around the propane canister.

Sonny handed me a road flare.

"Do you know how to use this?" he asked.

"I've seen it done," I replied.

"Light it up and toss it in the back, all the way to the front so Arthur has time to pull the door shut. I'll do the same up here. We'll make sure that the Chinese never use this truck again, even if they do find it."

We did as we were instructed and then walked briskly to the stairs and began climbing back to street level. Karen pointed out a sprinkler system mounted on the rafters of each floor but, of course, with no power there was nothing to trigger them.

Just as we exited onto the street, there was a muffled boom beneath us. The propane canister had blown.

It was a clear night, a welcome respite from the snowy, overcast weather of the previous few days. There was a full, silvery moon, and it caught our attention, looking so big I felt I could reach out and touch it. With no cloud cover though, the night was extremely cold, and I was shivering despite my heavy parka as we walked the mile or so back to the academy.

Along the way, Sonny mentioned that a local street gang had been moving out of their normal territory since the Flu and might be a problem. I have to admit, I wasn't really paying too much attention. I should have, but I was more concerned about a Chinese military patrol happening upon us at any moment.

We stayed four days at the academy and would have stayed more if fate hadn't conspired to force our hand. Well – fate or dumb luck or God, or whatever you happen to believe in.

Sonny had been right. The day after we dumped the truck, there was a lot of radio activity from the Chinese along with choppers buzzing above Worcester and the roads leading in and out.

From what little Sonny and Brooke could understand from the radio chatter, a sweep through on Worcester by the military seemed imminent. We didn't have much choice, laying low seemed like the *only* thing to do. Besides, Sonny and his group had not yet decided if they wanted to come with us or not.

Giving them more time to decide seemed like the right thing to do.

Beside the constant worry that the Chinese might discover us, it was a great few days. We were able to recharge and recover from our injuries. I finally let on about my Kung Fu experience and, for the first time in over a month, I was able to practice and spar.

Sonny's crew were good, especially Arthur, who I could tell was on par with my own skill, possibly better (although I wouldn't admit it). I had a few sessions with Sonny, and he was way out of my league, on another level completely, in fact. By the fourth day, I was managing to hold my own against him, defensively at least.

Luke took the opportunity to practice his crossbow. All that gaming appeared to have come in handy. He was a natural, and with practice shooting at the Kung Fu punching dummies in the academy's long practice hall, he became absolutely lethal. He painted targets on them and was able to hit the bull's-eye every shot after just two days.

He even had time to craft his own arrows and apart from the painted finish and slightly more refined materials of the originals, I could barely tell the difference between his and the manufactured ones.

To say the least, I was in awe of his many skills and wondered what other talents he might have hidden behind that slightly goofy exterior.

The forced confinement had another benefit. Information. While foraging, two days before finding us, Sonny told us he and two of the others had met three survivors as they passed through Worcester. The three teenagers had also come up from Rhode Island, but from the city of Warwick. They were led by a headstrong girl who told Sonny that the Chinese were using children as slave labor to clear the city of its dead.

She had speculated that Warwick was their foothold in the state due to its sea access. It was useful information, and only confirmed our worst fears.

"What happened to them?" Brooke asked.

"Well, they seemed really decent kids and we invited them to stay but she wasn't interested. They were heading north to Canada."

Our four new mouths taxed the food supplies at the academy. Luckily, with each day that passed, the Chinese aerial activity lessened and if they had sent in ground patrols, we hadn't seen any. Sonny deemed it safe to head out and forage on day four.

"Would you and Luke be interested in going out on an expedition to get more supplies?" Sonny asked.

"Hell yeah!" Luke answered for both of us. "No offence but I would love to get out and get some fresh air."

"Okay, good. I thought you might. There are grocery stores a few blocks from the academy, and a couple carts of canned food would feed us all for a while longer. I'll sketch you a map."

It was decided we would go out that night under the cover of darkness.

"Remember not to cross Foster Street," Sonny said, as Luke and I prepared to slip out through the side door of the academy. "It's the turf of that gang I told you about, the Red Tigers."

"Okay."

Sonny handed me an assault rifle which had been taken from the Chinese soldiers who captured us. The rifle was heavy and designed in what I thought was a funny way, with the magazine and action located behind the grip and trigger. It was a style Luke called 'bull-pup,' and he said it was the new, big thing in assault weapons. It was supposed to offer better control or something.

Luke rejected the rifle Sonny offered him and held up his crossbow.

"Quieter," he said simply at Sonny's raised eyebrow and showed him the handful of crossbow arrows he had in the large pocket of his parka. Old fashioned it may have been, but it looked plenty deadly in the cold light of the open doorway.

Sonny gave me a quick run through on how to operate the weapon. He showed me the selector switch, which was currently set on '1'; the other settings were '1' and '2'. He told me on setting 1, the gun shot one bullet at a time; on 2, it shot a three-round burst; and on 3, it was probably fully automatic, meaning I'd burn through my ammo with one squeeze of the trigger … and that the gun would be a bitch to control.

Sonny sounded so confident that he knew what he was talking about, I took it as gospel. In the end, he turned out to be *almost* right. I switched the selector over to '2' before we left the alley; if there was trouble a three-round burst would be more than adequate.

"It's freaking cold out here tonight, dude," Luke said, carefully stepping around a sheet of ice on the sidewalk. We were dressed in our normal clothing, although I had added a stocking cap under my parka's hood because it was another clear and very cold night.

"Yeah," I said, watching my breath plume.

I had one slip and only caught myself at the last moment. The black ice on the concrete was almost invisible.

"I hope these stores aren't completely looted," I said, concentrating more carefully on the path ahead. "I'd hate to think we're wasting our time."

"Sonny seemed confident," Luke said. "I don't think he'd send us out if he didn't think there was a good chance of us getting something."

"He could be hoping," I replied. "But that can be dumb sometimes."

"Man, everyone's gotta have hope. It's what keeps us going."

"Well, every time I find myself hopeful, everything turns to shit," I said, not sure why my mood had darkened.

"You're hopeful of getting to the safe haven," Luke pointed out, with a grin. "That tells me that you still have some hope."

"Well, I guess," I said. "But I have my doubts we'll ever get there. Between wild dogs, psycho traitor kids and the Chinese army, I don't think our chances aren't that great."

"Okay Debbie."

"Huh?"

"Debbie Downer."

"Oh, yeah. Funny. Look do I want to get to the safe haven? Yes, of course I do. Do I expect that I will? Well, look what happened to Sarah. That sort of thing could happen to any of us at any time."

Luke was quiet for a moment.

"Have you ever heard of Pandora?" he asked finally.

"The internet radio thing?"

"No, the legend," Luke said. "A long time ago, there was this dumbass giant, Epimetheus, who wanted a wife, so the gods made him the perfect woman. Her name was Pandora. Now, this dumbass giant had been given a magical box, like a golden chest or something. The king of the gods told him that it must never, ever be opened. After Pandora became his wife, the first thing Epimetheus did was show her the box and tell her it must never be opened.

"Well, telling someone not to do something only makes them want to do it, and all she could think about was what treasures might be in that box. So, one night while Epimetheus was fast asleep, Pandora crept down to the treasure room and decided to take the tiniest peek at what was inside the box. As can be expected, it didn't turn out so well – when the gods decree that something shall not be opened, you damn well wanna keep it closed."

"Okay, you have my interest," I said. "What was in the box?"

"Pandora opened the box, just a crack so she could take a peek, but the box was flung open by the force of what it held inside ... all kinds of monsters, plagues, pestilence, and disease came flooding out of it. All of the evils of the world followed by old age and death, two things the world had never known to that point.

"Imagine that ... living in a world where there was no sickness, no growing old, no death, and to suddenly have eternal, blessed life snatched from you!

"Anyway, all the evils of the world escaped the box, leaving only one thing behind. Looking into the now emptied box, Pandora spied 'hope', lying at the bottom. Before then, without the adversity of the things that had been trapped in the box, there had been no need for 'hope'. So, I guess the moral of the story is that there's only a real need for hope when things are at their darkest."

"I'm impressed, you actually managed to turn your story into a metaphor appropriate for our situation," I said.

"Well, of course, was that not my intention?" he said in a deep, theatrical voice.

"That's some heavy-duty mythology there, Luke. Did your parents read you a lot of books when you were little?"

"Nope, it was actually the background story for Goddess of Vengeance 2," he said with an impish smile and shrugged. "It seemed appropriate."

"I should have spent more time playing video games. I didn't know they were educational."

"Well, it's not like all I ever did was play games," he said, somewhat defensively.

"Sorry," I laughed. "I wasn't totally taking the piss. Games seem to have taught you a lot about coping with situations like this."

"I guess," he shrugged. "Most of it doesn't transfer that well to real life. The old 'real life' anyway. It's a pity that part of my life is over."

"Yeah, a pity for all of us ... hey there's a Honey Farms store! Want to try that first?" I asked, pointing at the convenience store sign. "It's not actually a grocery store, but I guess we don't have to worry about paying higher prices."

"Sounds good to me, Chief," Luke said, adjusting his course.

Honey Farms was about halfway down the block, past a line of silent cars. The frozen snow and ice on the windows of the cars kept us from seeing inside of them, so we watched them warily as we trooped on past.

A similar line of cars was parked on the far side of the street. I wondered, much like I had back in Fort Carter, if any of these cars might have frozen corpses in them. Just sitting where they succumbed to the Flu. I thought about knocking the snow off some windows and looking in, but decided against it.

No reason to disturb the dead, if they're there, I thought. Besides, I had creeped myself out enough.

The glass of the door to Honey Farms had been busted out, so it was not difficult for us to get inside. There were no shopping carts, but we found a rack of cloth grocery bags and each grabbed two.

It looked like a bunch of kids had ransacked the place. The chip and candy aisles had been demolished, but the limited range of canned soups and vegetables had hardly been touched.

Luke kept a lookout while I loaded my bags first. I packed cans of chicken noodle soup and peas. I had almost filled the two bags when I spotted some cans of creamed corn on a higher shelf. I took out some of the peas to make room and replaced them with the corn.

I've always had a thing for creamed corn. I realize it is a funny quirk to have, but I love the stuff.

While Luke was loading his bag, I wandered up toward the front door to keep watch. A big, half-moon was out in the clear sky, illuminating the road nearly as well as streetlights would have, if they'd been working.

I hadn't been standing there long when movement caught my eye. I ducked down, peering over the sill and watched in surprise as a girl pulled herself out from under a car across the street and scampered down an alley.

I didn't get a great look at her, but she looked to be about the same age as Luke and me. She was wearing a yellow rain slicker, not good for stealth at all.

"Should we go after her?" I asked, without taking my eye off the opening to the alley across the street.

"Go after who?" Luke responded, looking up from his half-full grocery bag.

"There's a girl across the street. She just went down that alley," I said.

"A girl? Did it look like she needed help?"

"Well ... we are in the deserted remains of a city, and she just crawled out from under a car in the freezing cold," I said. "I'm guessing she might need help."

"If she needs it, I'm all for helping her, man," he said, leaving the half-packed bag and walking up to the door where I stood.

"Okay, we'll go ask if she wants help," I said, setting my own grocery bags down. "Maybe bring her some of that hope you've been talking so much about. We can grab the bags on our way back."

We left the store and ran across the street to the mouth of the alleyway. The buildings crowded close together above it, dimming the moonlight.

"You sure she went in here?" Luke whispered.

"Yeah."

"Okay, let's go."

Luke took the lead, entering the alley with me close behind him. We hadn't gotten very far when we heard a scream from behind a dumpster about halfway down the alley.

"I guess she does need help," said Luke, cocking his crossbow and taking off. I unslung the automatic weapon Sonny had given me and we rushed down the alley doing all we could to avoid slipping on the thin sheen of frost that seemed to cover everything.

As we approached the dumpster, we slowed and heard the sounds of a struggle and loud laughter. We had almost reached it when my foot struck an old soda can I hadn't seen. Luke and I froze in place as first one, then another figure stepped out to confront us.

22

They were both Asian, wearing black leather jackets emblazoned with red tigers in the act of springing. Gangbangers. The guy on the right held a baseball bat with several long nails through it, and the other one was holding a knife.

Seeing our weapons, the one with the knife quickly reached inside his jacket.

"You kids better get lost!" snapped the guy with the bat, who appeared to be the older of the two as he put his hand on the other one's wrist, preventing him from pulling out whatever he had reached for. "This is Red Tiger turf."

"Help!" came a desperate cry from behind the dumpster followed by what sounded like a slap.

I took a step forward and the one with his hand in his pocket pulled out the gun he had reached for.

"Don't take another step, bitch!" he barked.

I heard a snap beside me and suddenly the aggressor gasped, looking down in disbelief at the crossbow bolt buried deep in his chest. The pistol clattered to the frozen pavement as the guy fell to his knees, before pitching forward.

"Holy shit!" the stunned man with the bat said, echoing my own thoughts. He took a step back as

Luke calmly loaded another bolt into the flight groove of his crossbow, cocked it and aimed it at him.

"You shot him! Jack! He shot Sammy!" he called to whoever was still behind the dumpster.

"Drop the bat," said Luke calmly.

We heard a squeal followed by a curse and another slap. The sound of struggling behind the dumpster came to an abrupt halt and a short, wiry guy stepped partially into view, careful to keep the dumpster between us and him. Like the other two, he was Asian. Chinese-American, for sure, given that he looked to be in his twenties and was not dead of the flu.

He held his hands up, but I could tell by the look on his face he wasn't surrendering, simply sizing us up. He had a small machine gun on a strap over his shoulder, the kind you see commandos use in old war movies. He looked like he'd seen plenty of hard life before the Flu and a ragged scar ran up the right side of his face. He was intimidating, to say the least. After glancing down at the guy on the ground, he looked up at us, anger in his eyes.

"Which one of you fuckers shot Sammy?"

Apparently, he had sized us up and found us lakking. His right hand curled around the handle of his weapon.

"I asked a question," he yelled.

"It was him, Jack," said the other gangbanger, his hands still up, at least until he saw which way things were going to go.

I tensed as Jack raised his gun toward Luke.

I had never actually shot a person deliberately before and I didn't mean to start right then, but things sort of got away from me. I meant to put a three-round burst into the pavement by his feet, to scare him off, but, well, the selector was set to 2. You see, Sonny had been wrong about the settings – 3 was actually the setting that gave a three-round burst, while 2 was full machine gun rock-n-roll.

Many people don't realize that a weapon firing on full automatic is not nearly like it is in the movies. In reality, it is very hard to control a weapon on full auto. Specifically, the combined recoil of all of the shots going off tends to cause the barrel to rise. Which is exactly what happened.

The first few rounds hit the pavement between Jack's legs, just as I had planned. But as the shots kept coming, the barrel kept rising and walked the remaining rounds of my magazine up his right leg. They struck him from just below the knee up to his right hip and into his abdomen before I was able to release the trigger. He hit the ground hard, dropping his weapon as he went.

My mouth dropped open.

Jack's right leg and side were a bloody, smoking mess. My ears were still ringing from the roar of the gunfire as the man with the bat dropped it and turned, running away like a mad man. He jumped the high fence behind him as if his life depended on it.

"Holy shit, dude!" Luke said.

I looked at my weapon in horror and let it drop from my trembling hands. Jack was screaming in agony, holding his leg to try and stem the bleeding. I stumbled to the wall of the alley and threw up the beans and franks I had eaten for dinner.

Luke kicked Jack's gun away and rounded the dumpster. I took a few moments to compose myself, and wiping my mouth on my sleeve, followed him.

The girl in the yellow slicker was slumped against the side of the dumpster. She was out cold, with her slicker open. The dirty sweatshirt underneath had been pulled up, exposing her belly and bra. Luke pulled her shirt down and buttoned up the slicker.

"You can see what that bastard was going to do," Luke said, taking in my pale face. "You did the world a favor by blowing his ass away."

"I know," I said, nodding my head and looking back at the gravely wounded gang member. He had stopped screaming and was unconscious or … worse. "I didn't mean to do it like that though…"

Luke didn't seem fazed by the fact that he, had just killed someone and I respected his sense of purpose. He un-cocked his crossbow and slung it over his shoulder before leaning over the girl.

"I'll carry her. You grab your gun and we'll go back and get the groceries we already bagged up," he said, putting her over his shoulder and standing up. "Let's get the hell out of here before bat-boy comes back with reinforcements."

"What about him?" I asked, after I picked up the automatic.

"There's nothing we can do about him now. In fact, I think he's dead, man."

I looked more closely and saw the gangbanger's chest was still. I nodded solemnly, and we started walking.

"You okay carrying her?" I asked, when we reached the end of the alley.

"Yeah, she's actually not that heavy," he said, flashing me a smile. "Just awkward to carry."

The trip back to the academy was done with as much haste as we could muster and with constant glances over our shoulders to make sure we were not being followed. We kept to the shadowed side of the street, staying out of the moonlight as much as possible.

We had to stop so Luke could rest several times, but each time, he refused my offers to take a turn. He obviously knew I was in a state of shock and I certainly didn't feel 100 percent, so I didn't protest.

We saw no signs of pursuit.

"I think we need to consider moving our departure time up," a puffing Luke said, as we stood by the back door of the academy, waiting for somebody inside to answer our knock.

"Yeah, tomorrow night, or the night after, at the latest. I'll talk to Sonny."

"Talk to Sonny about what?" Brooke said, as she pulled open the door. "Here now, who is that?"

"A damsel in distress," Luke said, grunting as he took the step and squeezed past her.

"We're probably going to have to leave within few days. I think we just poked a hornet's nest," I answered Brooke's first question as I squeezed past her.

After handing off the bags of canned goods to John in the kitchen, I stopped by the bathroom and washed my face. I didn't look any different, but I felt like a killer. I went to the main practice floor where Luke had lain the girl on a mat.

Sonny knelt over her, checking her eyes, while Ben, Brooke, and Allie looked on. Luke was standing to the side, massaging his neck.

"I guess she was heavier than I thought," he said.

"Is she going to be okay?" asked Allie.

"I think she probably has a concussion," said Sonny. "We'll know more when she wakes up."

I knelt beside him.

"No worse than that?" I asked.

"Can't tell yet," Sonny replied. "Her eyes are dilated, but not too much. I don't think the concussion is too bad, but once she wakes up, we better keep her from sleeping for a while." He looked at me. "Luke told me what happened with the Tigers. Do you want to talk?"

"Thanks. Maybe … not now."

"Okay," he said, and stood up. "We'll need to talk about the Tigers later. But, for now, I'm going to go get an extra blanket and pillow for our guest. If she wakes up, don't let her fall back asleep."

"Okay, I'll watch her if the others want to eat."

"Sounds good," said Luke. "I'll eat then come back and relieve you."

"Okay thanks," I said, and looked closely at her for the first time as the others filed out.

I guess to say she was beautiful would be a stretch; she had an ugly purple welt on the side of her face and was covered in dirt and grime. But none of that, not even the fact that her chestnut colored hair had been crudely hacked down to a few inches, could hide her girl-next-door beauty.

Beneath the rain slicker, which looked fairly new, her clothing was ragged, threadbare in some places, and it didn't take a genius to work out she'd been living pretty rough. I wondered how she could have survived on nights like this. The cold alone should have killed her.

I checked her pockets but found no sort of wallet or identification, just a key to what looked like a gym locker and a half-eaten bag of gummy worms. I put them back where I found them and settled down to wait for Luke.

About five minutes later, she moaned softly and turned her head.

"Is she coming to?" Luke asked, drifting back into the practice room.

The girl opened her eyes and looked around groggily.

"Are you all right?" I asked, leaning over her. "Are you awake?"

Her gaze fell on me, she had the most beautiful green eyes I'd ever seen.

"Well my eyes are open, aren't they?" she said, smiling.

And that is how I met Indigo.

23

Indigo, what else can I say about her. As her eyes looked back into mine I felt the beginnings of something. I didn't have much time to contemplate it just though, because suddenly it was as though someone turned on a light in her brain and her smile disappeared.

I saw her tense and thought she was about to scream or hit me. I drew back to give her room. Brooke, who had come in behind Luke, rushed over and put a calming hand on the girl's shoulder.

Of course, she was wary at first. Who could blame her? Knocked unconscious during an assault, she woke to find strangers leaning over her, my face looming largest of all.

"It's okay," I said. "You're safe. My name is Isaac. We're not going to hurt you."

"I'm Brooke."

"And I'm Luke," my friend said as he leaned over her and waved goofily.

Slowly, she appeared to relax. Brooke helped her to sit up and asked if she would like some water. Our guest nodded and looked around the room as Luke darted out to get her a drink. I saw her eyes pause on the doors and windows.

"What happened?" she asked, when her eyes finally settled back on me. "Where am I?"

"You're at the martial arts academy, on Main Street," I said. "My friend Luke and I were out searching for food when we saw you. We rescued you from those guys that were ... bothering you and brought you here."

Her eyes widened at the memory.

"You know those guys were Tigers, right?" she said. "If you messed with them, they'll be looking for you. They're killers."

"Don't worry about it; I don't think they know where we are."

"You better hope so. They killed my cousin Chloe. They would have…"

I saw tears well in her eyes and I felt my normally icy heart begin to melt. I wanted to question her more about what happened to her cousin, but it could wait. First, we had to gain her trust and let her get over the shock of the attack.

I changed the subject.

"Are you hungry? We have some food here," I said.

I could see the calm way I spoke to her, and Brooke's kind touch, had begun to ease her fears. I hoped my offer of food would allay them even more.

"Yes, thanks ... I'm starving," she said, as Brooke helped her to her feet and started across to the old sofa Sonny had situated against the wall.

"Brooke, I'll go and get some food, if you want to stay with…"

"Indigo ... Indigo Buchanan."

"Indigo. Cool. I'll go and get you something."

I met Luke on the way as he returned with the water.

"So, what do you think, man?" Luke said, pausing in the hall.

"She's alone, and scared," I replied. "And really, who can blame her? She doesn't know us at all. For all she knows, we could be as bad as these 'Tigers.' She said they killed her cousin."

"You think they did?" Luke looked troubled.

"Yes. I believe her. You saw for yourself what they were like," I said. "Those guys were animals. Hopefully they never track us down or it'll be a fight to the death."

"No kidding, Chief," Luke said. "If they kill an innocent girl, what are they going to try to do to us for killing their people?"

"I'd rather we didn't find out," I said, shaking my head.

Luke headed back with the water and I went to the kitchen, looking through the supplies of canned goods until I found a can of Spaghetti Os. I put them in a bowl and grabbed a clean spoon.

My footsteps echoed on the wooden floor of the academy's quiet halls as I walked back and saw where Sonny and his students were. When we got back to the main practice floor, Brooke was still sitting with Indigo on the sofa. They were quietly talking to each other.

As cold and unappetizing as they must have been, Indigo was very pleased with the Spaghetti Os. She explained that it was her first meal in over 24 hours and was almost finished eating when Sonny entered the room with Karen and Arthur following behind.

Indigo's eyes widened in horror when she saw Sonny, so I quickly put my hand on her arm as she dropped the bowl and tried to rise.

"It's okay! Indigo, it's okay! This is Sonny, he's one of us."

Still looking freaked out, she slowly settled back onto the sofa. Sonny wore a wry smile as I introduced Indigo to him and the other two, but he chose not to comment.

"We turned the supply closet across from the bathroom into a room for our guest," Sonny said. "We put in a sleeping mat and some warm blankets, and you can stay there as long as you want."

"Thank you," she said.

"Aren't you worried that people will get jealous? Giving Indigo a private room when no one else has one?" Luke said, a goofy grin on his face.

"No," Sonny replied, seriously. "We all realize she's been through a horrible ordeal and may need some time to adjust. Karen here will show you to your room later, when you're ready to sleep."

We all made Indigo feel as welcome as we could, and I think by the time we all went to bed she knew she was in a safe place with people she could trust.

I woke up some time around midnight and couldn't get back to sleep. I decided to go and get something to eat. I made my way carefully through the tangle of sleeping bags and bodies on the floor of the practice room to the hallway and into the kitchen. Following my late-night snack of stale Saltines, I was on my way back to the practice room when I heard voices coming from Sonny's office.

One of the voices was Sonny. I didn't recognize the other. It was a woman's voice, with a faint Chinese accent. Intrigued and, I have to admit, a little alarmed, I stopped to listen. Now understand, eavesdropping is not really my thing, but once in a while curiosity and self-preservation will get the better of me. This was one of those times and I make no apologies.

"Why did you come here?" I could hear Sonny saying. "How could you just show up here after what's happened. After what your government has done?!"

"Sonny! Our people didn't want this. I didn't ..." the woman said, emotion clear in her voice. "Many of us are just as appalled by what's happened as the rest of the world. Some in the upper echelons of government even tried to stop it, but they were brutally suppressed."

"How can I trust a word you say? You work for them! Why shouldn't I just kill you now?" Sonny asked.

His thoughts echoed my own and I briefly thought of running to grab my rifle. I didn't. I knew Sonny could handle himself and something in the woman's tone stopped me.

"Please, trust me Sonny. By coming here, I have placed myself in great danger," she said, a hint of desperation in her voice. "If you ever felt anything for me at all, please, just listen to me."

"Alright, Huian, I'll give you five minutes," Sonny replied. "You better make the most of them."

"Thank you," the woman, Huian, said. "You and your students need to get out of here. The People's

Army is tired of losing trucks. They are planning to route an entire division to Worcester. In three days, if you are not gone by then, you will be rounded up and sent to a camp. That is, if you are not simply executed."

"So, that's what you came here to do? To threaten me? Who else knows about us?"

"No, that's not why I came here at all," she said. "I came here to warn you and help you if I can. No one else knows. I am on the New England intelligence team. I requested it especially. We track resistance and movement over the six states and there is a big red flag over this city. I saw the location and came here on a hunch. I knew the virus wouldn't have killed you but ... well I am just so glad I found you alive."

"How do you propose to help us?" Sonny asked, his voice softening a little.

"I can provide you with a truck and I can promise it will not be reported missing for 72 hours."

"Why would you do this for me?"

"What the People's Republic of China has done is inexcusable. There are those of us trying to fight it, even now, or at least make sure that it never happens again."

"That still doesn't explain why you would help me," Sonny said.

The woman said something I couldn't make out.

"What was that?" Sonny asked.

"I said, because I love you," she said, in a louder voice. "I have always loved you, Sonny, since the first day I met you."

"Then why did you go back, Huian?" Sonny said. "Why did you leave me?"

"It was my duty and, back then, I put my duty ahead of everything. Even love."

"And now? Isn't it your duty to turn us in?"

"Now I hold my duty to be a higher cause," she said. "It sickens me to think I ever put the needs of the People's Republic above my own, especially given the way they abused that trust."

"Well, thanks for the heads up, at least," Sonny said. "I hope you are not too offended that I don't welcome you back into my life with open arms. Too much water passed under that bridge and, besides, you blew it up on your way out the door."

"I know ... someday I hope to show you just how much you still mean to me. Until then, I just hope you accept what aid I can provide and keep yourself safe."

"If I decide to accept your help, where will you leave this truck?"

"The same parking garage where you burned the last truck, on the same level," she said. "We've had the garage under surveillance since we tracked the GPS locator on the truck you dumped there. I will order the surveillance withdrawn at noon tomorrow. You can pick up the truck any time after that."

"What about the GPS locator on the new truck?"

"Take this envelope; it has keys to the truck and instructions to disable the GPS unit. I already thought of that for you. When you're through with the truck, park it out of sight. Without an active GPS unit, it should be a long time before they find it."

"I don't suppose the truck will be preloaded with supplies?" Sonny asked, and I imagined the grin on his face.

"The gas tank will be full, but that's about the extent of what I can do safely. Once you get out of Worcester, stick to the more rural areas. The People's Army is focusing on cities at the moment. They're trying to get them ready for the first wave of repopulation; the government wants civilians to begin occupying North America within one calendar year."

"Damn them to hell," Sonny spat.

"I must be going; the longer I stay, the more danger there is I'll be missed. I hope you and your students find a way to remain free and if in the future I can help you again, I will."

I moved away from the door and crouched behind a display case. It was dark in the hall, but the moon was bright outside and pools of light were cast through the frosted windows.

I saw the owner of the voice, a tall attractive Chinese woman in a black uniform, come out of Sonny's office. She glanced up and down the hall before hurrying off toward the academy's lobby. If she saw me, her eyes betrayed no hint.

A few moments later, a thoughtful looking Sonny walked out of the office and headed toward the kitchen. When he was gone, I hurried back to my sleeping bag.

I wasn't sure of what to think about the conversation I'd overheard. On one hand, I was excited about the prospect of a clean truck to escape in, but I was also worried it might be a trap. I pondered it as I tried to sleep. Why would the Chinese woman, Huian, create such an elaborate trap if she already knew where we were?

I tried to think of everything I knew about China and Chinese history and, in the end, I decided the concept of logic was not foreign to them. Either she was genuine, or it was a trap for a bigger fish.

Maybe there would be an extra GPS transmitter on the truck and Huian hoped we would lead her to other groups of survivors. Maybe she already knew about the safe haven and hoped to use us to find it.

I decided to talk to Sonny about it, no matter how uncomfortable I felt about eavesdropping.

Part Four

DEATH COMES CALLING

24

The rest of the night passed uneventfully, and I awoke just as the first light of dawn came through the high windows overlooking the practice room. Brooke and Ben were already up and had left the room. Luke was awake but still lying snug in the comfort of his sleeping bag. I wondered if I should tell him about what I had heard the night before but figured it could wait until after I talked to Sonny.

"I'm surprised you haven't checked on Indigo already, man," Luke said, grinning, as I struggled to extract myself from my sleeping bag. "I saw the eyes you were making at her last night."

I felt myself redden but didn't bite.

"She's probably sleeping in till lunch," I replied. "Sonny told Allie and Karen to stay with her last night and keep her up till at least midnight."

Luke yawned, making no attempt to get out of his own sleeping bag or to pursue his friendly ribbing.

"Do you know where Brooke and Ben are?"

"I think they had something to do with Arthur and John this morning," Luke said. "Looking for supplies in the office building across the street or something like that."

"What kind of supplies do they hope to find there? Office buildings don't seem like a good place to look for food or survival gear."

"I couldn't tell you," said Luke. "Anyway, I don't have any plans this morning so I'm just going to lay here and sleep."

I stood up and stretched, working the kinks out of my muscles.

"Enjoy," I said to Luke, and headed out to find Sonny. I wanted to talk to him about his secret rendezvous well before noon when the woman had said the surveillance would be switched off.

Sonny's office was empty, so I wandered to the kitchen to find myself something for breakfast. Samara and Mark were already there, eating bowls of cereal moistened with condensed milk from a can. At 14, Mark and Samara were Sonny's youngest students. They could hold their own on the mat, but Sonny chose to not take them on missions because of their age and smaller size. They were nice kids.

"Is there any milk left in the can?" I asked, grabbing a bowl of my own from the countertop.

"Yeah, maybe a quarter of the can," Mark replied. He pushed the can of milk toward me as I sat down. Samara did the same with the box of cornflakes.

"Thanks," I said, fixing myself a bowl. The condensed milk had a much stronger flavor than the two percent milk I was used to putting on my cereal at the Foster's house, but it was still edible.

"Have you seen Sonny?" I asked.

"He went up into the attic early this morning," Samara said. "That's where we keep the training weapons. He goes there for alone time."

"Thanks," I said, and shoveled another spoonful of cornflakes into my mouth.

I found Sonny sitting in the lotus position, meditating in front of a stand holding a pair of nine ring broadswords of Chinese make. He looked up at me as I entered the room, his face placid. I looked around, taking in the racks of ancient weapons lining the walls.

Samara said the academy stored its training weapons here, but all of the weapons in the attic looked frighteningly real to me. There were long staves, short fighting sticks, spears, strange pole arms, nunchaku, daggers, and an assortment of Asian-style swords. A large corkboard on one wall held dozens of throwing stars and other shuriken.

"I've decided," Sonny said. "We should go with you and, in my mind, the sooner we leave, the better."

"Okay," I said, sitting opposite him. "I know about Huian. I overheard part of your conversation with her last night."

I half expected him to be angry at my spying and braced myself for an argument, but he just stared at me expressionlessly before nodding. Perhaps there is something to that meditation stuff after all.

"Did you overhear the offer she made to me? About the truck?"

"Yes. Do you think we can trust her?" I asked. "I'm worried it might be a trap, but it seems overly elaborate if she already knows where we are."

"The same thought crossed my mind," Sonny said. "That's why I came up here to think. I find meditation brings clarity when my mind is clouded. In the end, it seems to me we have to trust her. We have very little choice in the matter – stealing a truck is impossible with the army on alert."

"Yeah, I suppose you're right," I said. "When are we going to go get the truck?"

"We'll go this evening, as soon as it gets dark," Sonny replied. "We'll bring it back to the alley and load it tonight with the supplies we're bringing. I'll drive, wearing the Chinese uniform while the rest of you stay in the back. We shouldn't have many problems if she was being honest. We'll try and head off by noon tomorrow."

"That timeline sounds good to me," I said, going over it mentally. "I'll let Luke know. We'll come with you when you go to get the truck."

"You know, it could be dangerous," Sonny said. "Even if it's not a trap, that parking garage is in Tiger territory. After what you did when you found Indigo, they'll be on the lookout for you."

"I know, but everything is dangerous now. We won't let you down."

"Alright, you can come," Sonny said, nodding his head. "I want to bring at least one more person with us though. I think Arthur."

"Sounds good to me," I said. "I might head down and try to get more sleep. I didn't sleep too well last night, and it sounds like we're going to have another long night ahead of us."

"Okay, I'll try to come up with something more resembling a plan," Sonny replied. "I'll wake you up around noon and fill you in on the details."

25

Allie woke me around 11:30 to tell me that new girl, Indigo, was asking to see the guy who had rescued her. I said thanks and yawned much more nonchalantly than I felt. As soon as she had left I jumped out of the sleeping bag and ran to the bathroom to make myself presentable. This consisted mostly of patting down my sleep-tousled hair and shaking my head at the bruising around my eyes which had now faded to an ugly yellowish green.

I decided that I had done all I could and walked the short distance from the bathroom to the supply closet Sonny had given Indigo as a room. Strange, I felt more nervous than I had when we faced off against the gangbangers.

I knocked on the door.

"Come in."

"Okay," I said, and opened the door. I found her sitting on the folded mat that was her makeshift bed, warm blankets gathered around her legs. She looked up at me and smiled.

"Isaac, right?" she said. "I just wanted to thank you again. I say 'again,' but in all the hustle and bustle of last night I'm not sure I even managed to thank you the first time."

"Don't mention it, Luke did more than me. He even carried you back. Besides, we make a habit of rescuing damsels…" almost as soon as the flippant words were out of my mouth I thought of Sarah.

"Yeah, I know, I thanked him too," she said, and then, perhaps noticing the sadness on my face: "One day you'll have to tell me about these other damsels you've saved."

"Does that mean you plan on sticking with us then?" I asked, trying to not sound too desperate. The last thing I wanted to do was come across as some sort of lecherous weirdo.

"Yeah, if no one minds," she replied. "This place seems safe and comfortable …" she paused as she saw me bite my lip. "What is it?"

"You probably haven't heard yet, but we're kind of planning to leave the academy tomorrow morning some time, it's getting too dangerous here, we … we found out something and it means we have to get out, and quick. You can come with us, of course."

"Um … okay," she said, puzzled. "I guess I've got nothing keeping me here in Worcester."

I blabbed. I couldn't help it. Her attentiveness and soft nature just put me at ease. I ended up telling her about Huian's warning that the Chinese Army was sending a division to Worcester. I also told her about the offer of the truck and my fears it might be a trap. I even talked about travelling to the safe haven.

She seemed as excited as I was about the safe haven, especially as it was as close as just a hundred miles or so north of us. In the end, I talked to her for over an hour that day, about the future, but also about the past.

I found myself opening up to her and telling her about my life before the Flu. It seemed I wasn't good at keeping secrets from pretty girls, but it wasn't just that – even though I'd only known her for a few hours, I felt I could trust her with my life … and after what I'd already told her, I probably had.

She told me about her life, as well. She was born and raised in Worcester. Like myself, Indigo had just turned 15-years old; in fact, her birthday was two days before mine. While she had not been a total loner in school like me, she hadn't been one of the popular kids either.

From our talk, I began to realize just how smart she was. It became obvious that she was way more book smart than I was, yet she didn't seem to have that in-your-face smarty-pants attitude so many smart people have. She told me she had grown bored of school and had let her grades slip, despite the fact that she was perfectly capable of doing the work.

Too many missed days and late assignments had torpedoed her marks to the point where her near perfect test scores were not able to compensate.

Her family had been a large, tightknit family, with many aunts, uncles, and grandparents, along with a dozen or so cousins, all living in the same neighborhood. Despite this, Indigo was like myself, an only child … and now, she too was all alone in the world. She began to cry as she told me how close she had been to her cousin, Chloe, and I realized just how deeply it affected her when she was murdered by the Tigers.

It must've felt a lot like losing a sister.

I asked her what happened. I saw hot anger dry the tears in her eyes. They were gathering food in a small supermarket when three Tigers happened upon them. The Tigers were rude and suggestive to the girls, and Chloe, always the sassier of the two, had smart-mouthed the ringleader. He shot her. Just like that.

Indigo and the other gang members had stood frozen in shock before she took off and ran for her life. He shot at her as she escaped but missed, and she had managed to elude them until the day before. I felt a seething anger at the dumb cruelty of the gang.

Talking about it seemed to help, but I was relieved when the subject changed. Speaking of loved ones made me think of my own sister, Rebecca. I almost had trouble picturing her face in my mind now. Even the memories of my Mom and Dad were slowly vanishing in the same way, like old photographs fading to sepia in a forgotten shoebox.

For some reason, I even told her of Amy, my foster sister, and how she had tried to be like a big sister to me that last Christmas Day. I felt a hot rush of guilt about how unfriendly I had been on what was probably her last day alive.

Then I told her about Sarah.

Strangely, the loss of my real family and the Fosters didn't come close to feeling as fresh or painful as the loss of Sarah and I wondered if something was wrong with me, or if it was just the fact that, for the first time in my life, I had lost someone that was in my care. Someone who had looked up to me ... trusted me with her life.

"I think that's it exactly," said Indigo, putting a hand on my arm.

I felt a jolt of electricity at her touch and wondered if she did too. A knock on the door ended our intense conversation and Indigo withdrew her hand as the door opened and Karen stuck her head in.

"Sonny would like to see you in his office, Isaac," she said. "I already told Luke and Arthur. They'll meet you there."

"Thanks," I said, as she rushed off. I turned to Indigo. "I've got to go, but I'd like to talk to you some more sometime, if it's okay with you?"

"Sure," Indigo said. "I enjoyed our talk. It feels so good just to be talking about what happened and remembering the people we lost. It feels ... cathartic? I think that's the word."

I smiled. One thing Indigo and I had in common was a love of words. I even remember reading through a dictionary for fun during the seventh and eighth grades. It sounds nerdy I know, but it's a fond memory, especially given there are no schools now and won't be for a long time. No teachers, no students, nothing except survivors and invaders.

I got up and paused at the door.

"I don't know if Sonny has told the others about Huian yet, so maybe not mention that to anyone yet."

"No worries," she said, and gave me a wink.

I headed to Sonny's office with a skip in my step, her touch still tingling on my arm.

When I got to Sonny's office, I knocked and then walked right in. Arthur and Luke were already there. Sonny sat behind his desk, glanced up as I entered, motioning. Luke gave me a little salute, but Arthur didn't look up as he intently studied a spiral notebook open on Sonny's desk.

"So, I take it you came up with a plan?" I asked.

"Yeah, most of the details are written down."

"It looks solid to me, man," Luke said. "I just hope we don't run into any unforeseen trouble."

Arthur slid the notebook in my direction and I looked over the plan Sonny had outlined. It seemed simple enough, barring any trouble from the Tigers or a Chinese patrol, and getting the truck should be a piece of cake.

"So, what do you think, Isaac?" Sonny asked.

"I agree with Luke. It seems solid."

"So, when are we going to do this?" Luke asked.

"Yeah, I'd like to get it done and over with as soon as possible," Arthur said.

Sonny checked the watch on his wrist.

"We will leave here at 1600. Make sure you have your stuff ready."

"Want to head over to the kitchen and grab some lunch?" Luke asked, as we left the office. "There are a couple of cans of chili con carne back there with our names on them."

26

After a relatively hearty meal of cold chili con carne with beans, I grabbed a couple of mixed fruit cups and a spoon to take back to Indigo's room. I still had a couple hours to kill before we went to retrieve the truck, and everything I planned to take with me was already in a pile next to my sleeping bag.

With that in mind and remembering how good our earlier conversation had been, I was keen to talk with her some more.

Unfortunately, I found her already deep in conversation with Brooke and Karen. Not wishing to intrude, I gave Indigo the fruit cups and said I'd catch up later.

"That's very thoughtful of you Isaac," said Brooke with a wicked glint in her eyes.

I felt my face heat up a few notches and shrugged before closing the door on them a little too quickly. The sound of their cheeky laughter followed me down the hall.

Not knowing what to do with myself, I decided to go find Ben and ask him what they had been searching for in the office building. I figured if Brooke was back, he would be as well.

I found him in our sleeping area, playing chess against Luke and looking very frustrated. I settled in to watch the end of the game silently as Luke slowly dismantled Ben's defenses. After four moves, Luke declared checkmate and sat back with a satisfied smirk on his face.

Ben looked at the table in disbelief for a few seconds before holding out his hand.

"Good game," he said, looking like he had sucked a lemon as Luke shook his hand.

"So, did you guys find anything interesting in the office building?" I asked him.

"Not really, but I daresay we got what Sonny sent us there to get," he said. "Why he'd want all those toner cartridges is beyond me."

"Toner cartridges? Like from photocopiers?"

"Yes," Ben said. "Plus several reams of printer paper, and as many rolls of tape as we could find."

"Why would he want those?" I asked.

"Beats the hell out of me," Luke said, and rubbed his hands together. "I love a good mystery though. Hey, maybe he's starting a newspaper? The Post-Apocalyptic Times!"

"Hardy har har," I said. "I'm sure he has his reasons, so we'll find out soon enough."

"Are you going to take the rifle with you this afternoon?" Luke asked.

I felt a short stab of remorse as I remembered what had happened the last time I held the rifle. I knew the gang member I shot had deserved it, but emotionally I wasn't quite ready to take responsibility for ending another human life so brutally.

"I don't know. I was thinking about just sticking with a handgun on this one," I said, looking down at the chessboard.

I wondered if Luke felt the same way about the Tiger he had killed with the crossbow. In the time since, I've found the killing gets easier, but the twinges of regret or guilt never really go away. The circumstances don't matter really. It doesn't matter how bad the other person was, I always ask myself if maybe I could have done something different.

And I always remember.

"Do you want to play?" I asked.

"Naw, I already had my fun," Luke replied. "Maybe Ben wants to play and redeem himself."

"What do you say?" I asked Ben.

"Sure, I'm always up for another game," he said, reaching for the pieces to reset the board.

The sky clouded over during the day. This had the benefit of warming the night slightly, but at a cost. It had gotten darker earlier and there was no moonlight to see by.

Sonny, Arthur, Luke, and I cautiously made our way back to the parking garage, hugging the buildings and keeping to the alleyways and side streets as much as possible.

The Chinese Army was on all of our minds, but Sonny thought it was the Red Tigers we really needed to watch for. He was right.

The parking garage was well inside their territory, and they were bound to be angry about losing two members the previous day. Sonny seemed to know a lot about them, but I didn't think much of it at the time.

Thinking about the Tigers made me realize it was less than 24 hours since I killed another human being. I'm pretty sure he was the first; the looter I had shot in front of the Fosters' home had already looked sick. Maybe the leg wound had sped up his demise, but I'm certain it wasn't fatal.

The thought of coming across one of the friends of the Tiger I had killed chilled me in a way the cold night couldn't, and I was worried the others might suffer as a consequence of my actions.

We walked through the darkness in near silence, moving carefully, and by a circuitous route. It took us nearly an hour to reach the parking garage. As we arrived, the first flakes of a fresh snowfall began drifting down from the now completely dark sky.

The plan called for Arthur and me to stay near the parking garage entrance, out of sight from the street but where we could keep an eye on things. Sonny and Luke would continue to the truck, make sure everything was okay and disable the GPS using Huian's instructions before picking Arthur and I up on the way out.

Sonny and Arthur were dressed in their black clothes, while Luke and I wore normal clothes and parkas. Nodding farewell to Luke and Sonny, I found a car to crouch behind, which afforded me a good view of the entrance. Arthur followed the others as far as the stairwell leading to the other levels and faded into the shadows. I realize, of course, that he was not a real Ninja, but he sure did a good impression of one.

Five minutes passed with agonizing slowness. While I knew it must have been at least a little warmer inside the parking garage, I honestly didn't feel it. I was as cold as I'd been since we left my hometown. My fingers were like ice and I placed my pistol on the concrete floor and rubbed my hands together for warmth.

It had seemed dark outside, but now that I was crouched in the darkness of the parking garage looking toward the opening to the street, I understood just how much darker it was in there when I plainly saw four silhouettes appear in the entrance. My heart skipped a beat before starting to race.

Tigers. That much was clear – one of them was holding a spiked baseball bat.

Shit, shit, shit.

They were speaking but I was too far away to hear what they were saying. After a time, one pointed in my direction, and then towards the stairwell Arthur had disappeared into. Two of the figures split off and headed deeper into the garage – toward me, while the guy giving the orders and the fourth headed for the stairwell.

I tensed and, moving as slowly and quietly as I could, picked up the .38. I was comforted only a little by the cold, heavy weight of it in my hand.

The Tigers, including the one holding the nail-studded baseball bat, came directly towards my hiding position. As he got closer, I saw from his shape that it was the one Luke had christened 'Bat-boy' after our earlier skirmish.

With him was a taller, younger Asian teenager. Both of them had automatic pistols shoved in their waistbands. As they approached I slowly scooted around the vehicle, keeping it between us. The last thing I wanted to do was use my revolver. I knew any shots would bring their other two friends running and, if they were armed with guns too, I didn't like my chances in a four on one shootout ... or even four on two if Arthur came to back me up.

Daring to cast a quick glance in that direction, I saw the other two Tigers must have already entered the other stairwell. I took the relative silence from that direction as a positive sign they had not stumbled over Arthur, so I quickly switched my focus back to the other two. They had stopped no more than 10 feet away from where I crouched.

"Are you sure it was them?" the taller one asked Bat-Boy. "The bastards who killed Sammy and Jack?"

"At least one of them," Bat-boy said. "I recognized the jacket of the kid with the crossbow."

"Come on, let's keep going ... and keep an eye out. Chen doesn't want them to slip past us and get out if they hear him and Hammer on the stairs," he said. "We better not slip up. I've never seen him as mad as when you told him Jack was dead. I feel sorry for the poor son of a bitch who was stupid enough to kill his kid brother ..."

"Yeah, that little shit better hope he dies from a bullet, because if we capture his ass..." he slapped the nail-free part of his bat into the palm of his hand. I jerked at the loud slap and almost overbalanced.

Chen's brother? The way they were talking, Chen was obviously the leader. And it turns out I had killed his brother. No wonder they were so pissed.

The two Tigers started walking again and were soon far enough beyond where I crouched for me to relax a little.

That feeling was short-lived, however, when it dawned on me that Luke and Sonny were in real danger. I had no way of getting past the Tigers, either of the pairs, to give warning. Even if they finished with the truck and got it up and running before the Tigers got to their level, they would have to drive right by at least two of the armed thugs to get out.

I hoped Arthur had managed to get down the stairwell to warn Luke and Sonny before the two Tigers heading that direction had seen him. That would be something but getting out would still be a hell of a problem.

Looking into the parking garage toward where the two Tigers had vanished in the darkness, I strained and could hear the faint sound of their footsteps getting further away. When I judged them to be distant enough, I broke cover from where I was crouched and furtively moved to the stairwell.

I had been in the stairwell before, when we had left the garage after burning the first Chinese truck. The street level of the parking garage was the top floor; the other six floors were located underneath, so from here the stairs only went one direction – down into the darkness.

The stairs were located at the back of a small alcove with an elevator door in one wall. The stairs wound around the elevator shaft's column as they descended. There was a landing and an elevator door on each garage level.

I paused at the entrance to the alcove, listening for the sounds of the Tigers on the stairs. I didn't hear them, but I distinctly heard hurried footsteps coming towards me from behind.

I spun around and found a middle-aged Chinese man sprinting at me from the street entrance – he pulled a long carving knife out of his belt as he came.

Adrenaline kicked in, and, abandoning any notion of stealth, I brought up the revolver and squeezed the trigger twice. The booms echoed through the parking garage. The first shot missed; I've no idea where the bullet went. The second shot struck the onrushing man just above the sternum, about an inch to the left.

I expected him to be knocked backwards by the force of the shot – after all, it always happens that way in movies – but he just jerked slightly and kept coming. I stepped back against the wall, watching in disbelief as he steamed straight for me. The thought he might be wearing a bulletproof vest crossed my mind and I was preparing to fire again when, two steps later, his legs gave out and he slammed face down onto the cold pavement in front of me.

Hearing a noise in the alcove behind me, I spun again with my .38 raised in trembling hands. The elevator doors were being pried open. As they slowly parted, I saw the elevator car itself was stuck someplace between this floor and the one below. About a foot of the car could be seen along with its roof, and there crouched Arthur.

"Hurry up and get in here," he whispered fiercely. "Before every Tiger in the neighborhood shows up."

I heard running footsteps from the car park as I clambered up next to him and we worked to close the doors again.

"What about Luke and Sonny?" I asked, puffing with exertion.

"I already warned them. They should be hiding in the bottom of the shaft," he whispered as the doors finally met. Darkness, absolute and impenetrable, cloaked the elevator shaft when the doors closed.

"Keep your gun handy in case somebody tries to open those doors but try not to move around or talk too much. We don't want to give them a reason to search here."

It didn't take long before we could hear agitated voices talking loudly outside the elevator doors. Although we couldn't make out exactly what they were saying, the man I'd shot had been found. Not exactly surprising, since I'd left him lying out in the open.

Adrenaline was still coursing through me and I felt more than a little bit jittery, so much so, that when someone hammered on the door I pointed my gun in that direction and was about to squeeze the trigger. I felt Arthur's hand touch my shoulder.

"No," he said, his whisper barely audible in my ear. "Shoot only if you see light from the sliding doors opening ... and make every shot count."

The voices outside the elevator died down and, after a while, stopped altogether. I thought they had left to continue their search through the parking garage, or perhaps went out to comb the streets, thinking we'd slipped out after shooting their rear guard, but I couldn't be certain. For all we knew, there could be a Tiger standing in the alcove, waiting for somebody to stick their head out.

"Should we try the door?" I whispered to Arthur.

"No, too risky right now," he said, producing a small flashlight from the pouch on his belt. He flicked it on. The cone of light played over the walls and floor of the shaft, and then he pointed it up.

The building that the parking garage was located under was a four-story office building which had held mostly law offices and accounting firms, if the sign at the front was any indication. The shaft continued up into the building above although Arthur's torchlight didn't reach that high. It did, however, illuminate the elevator doors of the two stories above us.

"Do you think that they'll be searching for us in the office building itself?" I asked.

"I doubt it – not yet, anyway. The only door from the parking garage into the building lobby is closed off with a chain and a padlock. I found that out when Sonny had me scout this place when we were looking for places to dump the first truck we took. As long as the chain's in place on that door, they won't think we went in there and the stairs only lead down further into the parking garage."

"Do you think we can get up there?"

"I don't know," Arthur said. "I was hoping that there would be some sort of maintenance ladder or something, but there isn't. I don't think climbing the cables would be that easy and, even if we did, I'm not sure how we could get the doors open while clinging to them."

"I see what you mean," I said. "Although, the doors have rails they slide on ... maybe we could stand on the rails to one side of the door and push them open."

"Yeah, maybe..." Arthur said, not sounding convinced. "Another option would be to hide in the elevator car itself. There's an access hatch over there," he shone the light over to illuminate a trapdoor a few feet from where I crouched. "With the narrowness of the hatch, I don't think any Tigers checking the elevator shaft from above would look for us in there."

"Yeah, but if they did climb down and find us inside ... well, it would be like shooting fish in a barrel. Not sure I want to be a fish."

Arthur switched his light off and we squatted there in silence for a few moments. In my mind, it seemed the question was mostly theoretical, as we seemed to be safe where we were for the time being. The adrenaline was beginning to wear off and a vague sense of exhaustion was replacing the jittery excitement that I had been feeling.

"How long do you think we should wait before we do something?" I asked him.

"Let's give it another few minutes."

"Sounds good to me," I answered.

We waited silently, my brain working overtime as it cycled through the different ways this could end. Most of them bad.

Finally, Arthur whispered, "Okay, let's give it a hundred count."

"Okay."

I began to count upwards from one in my head. I took my time, carefully regulating my count speed with a Mississippi between each number. It was a long hundred seconds. We didn't hear a sound outside but that didn't ease the tension and fear I felt at the prospect of leaving our little sanctuary.

Arthur finished counting before I did, switching his flashlight on while I was still in the low nineties. Holding the light in his mouth, he stepped up to the door and began to pull it open. The inner door opened easily, but the outer door required more work and I began to appreciate just how difficult it had been for him to get in here, and then to allow me in later.

We got the outer door open a crack and I put my eye to it. I couldn't see anyone waiting to ambush us, so I gave Arthur a nod. We grabbed one door each and slid them open enough to allow us to get out. He hopped out first and I followed.

The stairwell alcove was empty, but the body of the man I shot had been pulled to one side.

"They'll still be around here someplace," Arthur said quietly. "The Tigers aren't known for giving up."

"That's not gonna help their mood either," I said, nodding my head toward the dead man regretfully. Now that we were back out of the pitch darkness of the elevator, I had to ask him something I was curious about.

"How did you know?" I asked. "How did you know I was going to shoot my gun in there? There's no way you could possibly have seen me in the dark."

"You stopped breathing," Arthur said. "Sonny taught me holding one's breath is often a sign that violent or stressful action is about to be undertaken."

"You must have super hearing," I said, pondering that a moment. "I wonder how he and Luke are doing."

"Well we haven't heard gunfire, so I guess they're okay for the moment. We can't think too much about it though, they'll have to handle it themselves. We have to decide what we're going to do."

"Yeah, what are you thinking?"

"As I see it, we have three options. We can try and make our way down to the truck and the others, we can bail and go back to the academy, or we can stay here and basically do nothing."

"Option two is out," I said. "I'm not going back while they're still in danger."

"If we stick to Sonny's plan, we should stay here, and wait for them," Arthur said.

"Luke likes to say that no plan survives first contact with the enemy," I said. "I think we'll need some revisions to Sonny's plan." I looked at the stairwell, and then toward the parking garage. "I think we should head down, but instead of the stairs we should go down the ramps. If we try the stairwell, there's always the chance we'll miss Luke and Sonny leaving in the truck. If we walk down the parking ramps and they happen to be on the way out, we can just jump in."

"Fine, if that's what you want to do, let's do it," Arthur said. He sounded a little peeved that I was taking control and tried to wrest it back. "We are going to move quick and quiet, stay low, and keep a good lookout. And, for God's sake, don't shoot anybody."

"I'll do my best," I said, shrugging my shoulders.

Creeping along the inner wall of the parking garage, we moved as swiftly as we could while still being stealthy. I knew I didn't want to be taken unawares by a couple of gangbangers and I was sure that Arthur felt the same way. Mom, my real mom, used to say if wishes were fishes, we'd walk on the sea, as a way of telling me that I wasn't always going to be able to get everything I wanted. Back then, when I was just a kid, I never understood what she meant. I do now.

We had just rounded the first turn in the garage when the guy with the bat stepped out from behind a car right in front of me. A shot of adrenalin sent my heart racing in my chest. I ducked as the bat whistled through the air where my head had just been, slamming into a car's fender, the nails denting and scratching the metal. I tried to bring the .38 up, but the gangbanger's foot caught me in the pit of my stomach and I was knocked backwards to the ground, the air whooshing out of my lungs. The revolver slipped from my grasp and skittered a dozen feet across the cold pavement.

"I got one!" he shouted, stepping over me as I lay gasping for breath. "It's the guy who gunned down Jack! I bet you wish you had a machine gun now, don't you bitch? You little punk ass bitch!"

He raised the bat, its wicked nails shining silver in the dimness of the parking garage. I held my hands up in a futile gesture of self-defense. *Shit!*

I closed my eyes as he swung and waited for the blow. It never came. Instead, I heard a grunt of pain and surprise.

I opened my eyes as the Tiger stumbled to one side, the bat now in one hand as his other struggled to reach around under his shoulder blade. Arthur was a few feet away, balancing on the balls of his feet but the Tiger was oblivious. His face, which had been etched with hate only a moment ago, was now pale. His eyes widened as he found what he had been reaching. I watched, hypnotized. Finally, he gained purchase on whatever he was reaching for and took a deep breath before jerking his arm violently.

He looked at the bloody object in his hand in disbelief. I had seen throwing knives like it before on the racks in the academy attic. While he was distracted, I started to slowly crawl backwards away from him. I needed that gun.

My attacker started to turn, as if he suddenly realized that if there had been a knife in his back, then…

Arthur hit the man with a vicious kick to the same place the knife had struck. Roaring with pain and stumbling with the force of the kick, the gangbanger turned to face him while swinging the bat one handed.

Arthur walked into the swing, and the thug's arm, rather than his bat, slammed into Arthur's side. Allowing this to happen was evidently part of Arthur's plan, because he then brought his right arm down to trap the wrist of the Tiger and at the same time gave him a brutal palm strike to the chin. Bat-Boy didn't even groan as he fell to the floor.

"Are you all right?" Arthur asked, as I scooped up the revolver and scrambled to my feet.

"Yeah, thanks," I gasped. I was trying to regain my breath and stood partially bent over while I sucked wind. "Is he dead?"

"Not yet," Arthur replied. "But we should finish him off before we move ..."

His words were cut off by three impossibly loud gun shots coming from behind the car to our side.

I dropped to the ground, and heard Arthur drop behind me. I scrambled to the car and peered under it, scanning for the feet of the gunmen on the far side. I couldn't see any.

"Are you okay?" I whispered to Arthur, still straining to see. "Arthur?"

I turned. Arthur was lying on his side, his eyes open and unblinking as a deep crimson, almost black, pool of blood formed around him.

"Shit ... Arthur?"

A scuffing noise brought me back to reality, and I quickly looked under the car again. This time, my gaze fell on a pair of red leather cowboy boots moving cautiously toward the car I was lying behind.

Figuring the other Tigers were probably already on their way, I decided this was it. I was going to go out in a blaze of glory. I aimed my gun at the cowboy boots and almost as if he wanted to be shot, the wearer stopped perfectly still, one leg behind the other.

"Roy?" he called.

I pulled the trigger. The roar of the handgun was deafening.

The bullet struck the Tiger wearing the cowboy boots in the right ankle and continued on through his left heel. There was a cry of agony as he collapsed to the concrete. His gun clattering away when he used his hands to break his fall.

The wounded man turned his head and his eyeballs locked onto mine. For a moment that stretched on forever, we stared at each other. I knew the fear I saw in his eyes was mirrored in my own.

He reached for his pistol.

I shot him in the forehead.

27

I'd taken my first human life less than 24 hours before, and now I'd taken two more. It seemed I was on a roll. Maybe I was responsible for another, as well, I reminded myself. Arthur.

I felt sick.

Arthur was only here because I had wanted to come this way. It may sound strange, but right at that moment, Arthur's death weighed on me more heavily than the lives I had actually taken. As I lay on the cold concrete in shock, I thought about Karen. If I managed to get back to the academy in one piece, I was going to have to tell her that Arthur was dead.

As I'd watched them together over the week, I remembered thinking how lucky they were to have each other as the world was falling apart around them. Now, because of my decision, Karen was going to have to face this shit-hole of a world alone. Is this really what being a leader is? Getting people killed with the choices I make? The thought frightened me. Who would ever willingly accept such a responsibility?

I waited a minute but didn't hear or see anyone rushing my way. Warily, I slowly pulled myself up into a crouch and peeked over the hood of the car. My luck ran out. In the gloom of the garage ahead, I saw two figures appear.

They were moving slowly, one holding some form of handgun and the other a rifle or shotgun, I couldn't tell which. I swung open the cylinder of my .38 and, with trembling hands, shook the four spent cartridges into my hand and carefully set them on the floor. In my pocket I found some new shells and reloaded the revolver. I was trembling so much as I closed the chamber that I was almost in disbelief that I hadn't dropped any shells.

Staying low, I moved toward the back of the car, trying to find a better position from which to make my last defense.

They kept coming, as bold as life, walking to the middle of the lot, slow and deliberate. They were about 20 yards away from where I looked over the trunk of the car, ready to duck if they aimed at me. I knew instantly that one of them was the leader Chen, the brother of the one I had killed in the alley.

How did I know? I'm not sure, except to say that his fearless and self-confident march toward my hiding place marked him as a leader. He was tall and well-built and despite the cold, wore a black, sleeveless muscle shirt.

"Don't come any closer," I yelled, trying to sound more confident than I was.

The man walking with Chen stopped instantly, but the leader sauntered on.

"Stop!"

This time he did, but not in a submissive way. He planted his feet, and kept his hands by his side, the shotgun pointed safely at the floor. I took in his hard face and slicked back hair. Then he laughed at me. Of all the things that I expected, this was not one of them. I felt myself redden; as a child I hated kids at school laughing at me when I wasn't in on the joke. It had made me feel weak and stupid. In the vulnerable state I was in right then, his scorn succeeded in doing just that.

"Well, what have we here? A little man with a big gun. Why don't you come out and we'll talk about all this nonsense?"

He actually sounded reasonable and I almost stood up, but then I spotted his buddy take a step.

"I said stop!" I yelled and fired a warning shot into the air. It hit the concrete above me and the bullet ricocheted dangerously close. As the chips of concrete and dust fell onto the car, I was gratified to see a look of uncertainty flash across Chen's face as he waved the other man back.

"No need for that, little man," he said smiling. "I just want to talk to you. I believe you knew my brother?" Unexpectedly, he crouched and put his shotgun on the floor. When he stood he began to walk toward me again, this time with his hands up. I raised my gun and pointed it at his head.

"Now, now. You wouldn't shoot an unarmed man, would you?"

He judged correctly. I wouldn't – couldn't – shoot a man who was unarmed with his hands up. My gun hand was shaking, and I knew he could see it.

"Stop ... I said stop."

It sounded weak and he didn't stop.

"It's okay, we're just gonna talk, little man," he whispered, as he reached the other side of the car. I felt like I was under the control of a snake charmer. I knew he was lying. As soon as he was within reach of me I was as good as dead.

That was when the truck screeched around the corner behind them and the parking garage was flooded with light. Chen spun around as the fast-moving vehicle sped toward us.

Chen's partner raised an arm to shield his eyes from the bright headlights as the rifle in his hands barked. He was too slow. The truck struck him and, even though it was a glancing blow, he flew off to the side like a rag doll as the truck came barreling on. Chen was a lot quicker. He glanced at me, the soothing look on his face transformed into one of venomous hatred.

"Not over, bitch!" he spat, before sprinting to the safety of the stairwell. The truck locked up its brakes and screeched to a stop beside me. The passenger side door opened, and Luke held out his hand.

"Hurry up, get in!" he yelled. "Where's Arthur?"

I grabbed Luke's arm and he helped pull me up into the cab. A rifle shot sounded behind us and we heard the ping of a bullet ricochet off the back of the truck.

"Where's Arthur?" Sonny repeated, glancing over from the driver's seat.

"He ... he didn't make it," I replied, a sob escaping my throat. Sonny's face spasmed in anger before he stepped on the gas again and we lurched off. I nearly fell out as we took the corner fast, but Luke gripped me tight and managed to pull the door shut as we careened down the ramp.

I heard a number of shots ping into the back of the truck, but we met no more Tigers as we roared out of the parking garage and skidded onto the icy street. Sonny drove erratically, taking random turns, I assumed in order to confuse any pursuit, but he soon began to slow down.

"Sonny, what are you doing, dude?" Luke asked, looking at our driver.

With my hurried entrance into the cab of the truck, Luke had shuffled across and was right next to him now. Not only was Sonny driving slower, but he was hunched over the wheel and seemed to be having trouble keeping the truck straight.

"Is there something wrong with the truck?" I asked.

"No, the truck is fine," he gasped. "Can either of you drive? I've been shot."

End of Book 1

America Falls continues in Book 2

On The Run

ABOUT THE AUTHOR

Scott Medbury is a husband and father of four, who has a keen interest in finance, geo-politics and human society.

Scott's works have been published in 18 countries around the world and he has sold over half a million books worldwide.

His fascination about man's place, future and conduct in an overcrowded, rapidly changing world and these themes form the backdrop for his action packed but thought provoking America Falls Series.

You can sign up to his newsletter at
www.scottmedbury.com.